THAT
TIME I GOT
KIDNAPPED

Books by Tom Mitchell

HOW TO ROB A BANK

THAT TIME I GOT KIDNAPPED

THAT TIME I GOT KIDNAPPED

TOM MITCHELL

HarperCollins *Children's Books*

First published in Great Britain by
HarperCollins *Children's Books* in 2020
HarperCollins *Children's Books* is a division of HarperCollins*Publishers* Ltd,
HarperCollins Publishers
1 London Bridge Street
London SE1 9GF

The HarperCollins website address is
www.harpercollins.co.uk

1

ISBN 978–0–00–829226–3

Tom Mitchell and Euan Cook assert the moral right
to be identified as the author and illustrator of the work respectively.

Typeset in Plantin by
Palimpsest Book Production Ltd, Falkirk, Stirlingshire
Printed and bound by CPI Group (UK) Ltd, Croydon CR0 4YY

A CIP catalogue record for this title is available from the British Library.

To Mum and Dad

PART 1

TUESDAY

TIME UNTIL THE MOVIE SHOOT:

45 HOURS 30 MINUTES

Snowmageddon
Heathrow Airport, Greater London

If my journey across America taught me anything, it's that I'm no hero. I worry too much for one thing.

And so spending the day before the flight watching *Top Ten Plane Crashes* on YouTube wasn't the *best* idea. And, being driven to Heathrow through the gloom, I could've done without Amy, my sister, miming explosions and mouthing booms of fiery air.

On the M4, in order to stop worrying about the plane breaking apart over the Atlantic or imagining the view of the endless sea roaring up to my window, I tried reigniting my excitement about what waited for me in America: FORTUNE AND GLORY.

(For real and for sure. 100 per cent. No sweat.)

Background: I'm not saying I'm mad about Marvel but here are the facts. I'm fourteen and I've got a Spider-Man bedspread. (Not many people know this.) My walls are covered in Spider-Man posters and the password to all my accounts is PeterParker62. I'd probably get a Spider-Man tattoo, something subtle on my shoulder, if I didn't know for a fact that Dad would laser it off himself, Cyclops-style, as soon as he found out.

I'm not one of those obsessives, though, so don't judge me. Part of the problem is that I live in Somerset, where, according to Google, the last exciting thing happened in 1998.

What I'm trying to do here is help you understand the mind-blowing excitement experienced when I received an email from Marvel Studios saying I (me, Jacob Clark) had won the chance to be an extra in a new movie shooting in Hollywood, *and*, wait for it, with all my flights and accommodation paid for.

There was a worrying moment when I thought Mum and Dad wouldn't let me go, like with the Year Seven Adventure Weekend after Mum had read about sheep ticks, but as soon as the local newspaper rang to ask if they could report my success they were sold. We FaceTimed the grandparents and everything.

'My son in a film,' Dad said more than once in a weird tone of voice I hadn't often heard.

This wasn't all my birthdays and Christmases coming at once but everybody's birthdays and Christmases for the rest of eternity.

The worry, aside from my plane maybe crashing, was that I didn't know *which* superhero the film would be about. Supposedly it was all top secret. Twitter didn't have a clue. Amy kept saying it'd be 'Idiot Boy' but the joke was on her because there's no superhero called that.

Inside the terminal, a huge screen, listing destinations I'd only heard of in Geography, said my flight to Chicago was on time and leaving from Gate B41. Dad reckoned I'd not been booked on a direct flight to LA because that would have made the ticket more expensive. (He'd not left the country since the disastrous Calais 'booze cruise' all the way back when I was in primary school – a fact he was weirdly proud of.)

We headed straight for security because there'd been a crash near Swindon, which left no time for messing about. Dad handed over my suitcase. It was pink and had, in glittery white writing, the word PRINCESS across its front. Back home, pulling the bag from the attic and coughing only slightly from the dust, Mum had said there was no reason why boys couldn't have pink suitcases and it was perfectly fine and, anyway, there'd be no losing it.

'It's 2020, Jacob,' she'd said, and although she was right I didn't know what the year had to do with anything.

She'd also said the Princess was exactly the right size; it could hold all my clothes and still qualify as 'carry-on'. Proper travellers never bothered putting their bags in the hold these days supposedly.

'It's the internet for you,' said Mum.

(She used the internet to explain a lot of things.)

Dad shook my hand and pulled me in for a hug. He ruffled my hair, instructing me to stay safe. Mum had her puppy eyes when she squeezed me and said she was missing her little soldier already.

As she released me she handed over what I thought was a note with emergency numbers and instructions about what to do if I ripped my jeans etc. She closed her hand over mine and put a finger to her lips. As I shifted the paper to my pockets I saw it was American money – a bill with '100' in the top corner. My imagination exploded with fireworks of possibility. How much Marvel merch would that buy?

(Answer: not much. But it didn't matter because the studio was also giving me spending money.)

Mum read from her phone a list of things I shouldn't do:

1. Lose my passport.
2. Miss the plane.
3. Agree to carry things for strangers, especially friendly men with beards.
4. Eat or drink (American) things if I wasn't sure what they were.
5. Loiter.
6. Flush the plane toilet without the seat being down.
7. Forget to exercise my legs and get deep vein thrombosis.
8. Allow myself to be distracted when leaving the plane.
9. Lose the instructions about the connecting flight.
10. Miss the connecting flight.

'Understood,' I said. 'Thanks, Mum.'

'Do you want me to write them down for you? I'll write them down.'

I told Mum that it was fine and she didn't need to write them down.

'What was number five, then?' asked Amy, suddenly present.

'Loiter?' I asked.

Mum beamed. Dad nodded. Amy yawned.

'And make sure you ring as soon as you land,' they said in stereo.

I crossed my heart and hoped to die, which I instantly regretted.

It was Amy's turn to say goodbye.

She chewed gum and Mum told her to take her earphones out, for heaven's sake.

'Hope you don't crash,' she said, smiling.

'Amy!' said Dad.

'What?' She shrugged. 'I do. What's wrong with that? It'd be bad to say I *wanted* him to crash.' She narrowed her eyes. 'Have you seen the weather in Chicago, by the way? It looks intense.'

Suddenly her phone was in her hand and she was holding its blinding screen to my face. I couldn't take in the detail before Mum had fussed it away but what I *did* read was a single word: Snowmageddon.

Not 'Paradise' or 'Perfect Landing Weather'.

No.

Snowmageddon.

'Is that even a word?' I asked.

'Ignore your sister,' said Mum as my chest buzzed

with anxiety bees. She brushed my fringe from my forehead. 'I can't believe I'm putting my little boy on a plane. On his own.' She turned to Dad. 'Why don't we all buy a ticket? We could put it on the credit card. When was the last time we had a holiday? What about *my* wellbeing?'

She looked around frantically for someone she could buy a ticket from.

'Remember Calais,' said Dad to Mum, before turning his Dad-stare on me. 'Don't miss your connecting flight. You hear? Don't. Miss. Your. Connecting. Flight. I don't want to have to drive to Chicago to rescue you.' I frowned. Amy yawned again. 'You know what I mean.'

I didn't. But I *did* know that I wasn't a kid and that everything would be 100 per cent fine.

'I'm not a kid,' I said, sounding about as convincing as a nativity play. 'Everything will be a thousand per cent fine.'

'Just make sure you stay safe!' said Mum, her smile looking like it had been branded on to her face. 'Speak to a police officer if you get lost.'

'And don't miss that connecting flight!' added Dad.

CHAPTER 2

'You're Welcome, Princess'
Chicago, Illinois

I missed the connecting flight.

(But I swear it wasn't my fault.)

A woman who looked like she sold make-up at Superdrug walked the aisle before the plane landed and wrote out what I had to do. It was all very straightforward, she said. She spoke with a British accent, which steadied my trembling. A bit.

(I'd like to have the power not to get worked up about stuff like this. Maybe 'power' is not the right word. Maybe I mean 'confidence'?)

She said I'd have to go through security again because 'that's how they do things in the States', sigh. I'd also have to pass IMMIGRATION before getting to the connecting flight. Then I should follow the arrows pointing towards . . . CONNECTING FLIGHTS. I also had a couple of forms to fill out, which she could help me with after she'd tidied the cabin, and had I seen the vomiting baby? What a flight!

'So, in conclusion, all very straightforward,' she said, sighing again.

Even though it didn't sound very straightforward, I nodded and said thanks. She was not only cabin crew but also adult – the combination meant she knew what she was talking about. Also, she smelt like a movie star or, at least, what I imagined one would smell like. Sweet and flowery.

I've always trusted nice-smelling people.

(Arrows would be the same in America, wouldn't they? They wouldn't mean the opposite? Because they drive on the other side?)

The plane descended. The clouds broke. America spread out like a tablecloth. But one from a black-and-white film. Because Amy had been right about the snow – it covered everything and what it didn't cover was concrete. There were no skyscrapers, no yellow taxis. The US of my imagination had looked more exciting. Here there was grey. And there was white. And that was about it.

Snowmageddon.

The captain thanked us for flying British Airways. He suggested we wrap up warm and also made a joke about the runway looking like an ice rink, which didn't help my nerves. Or those of the suit sitting next to me.

(She swore. And apologised for swearing. And said she'd have had more wine if she'd known about the ice. Because she didn't want to die sober, she said. And then apologised for saying all this to a kid.)

I cleared my throat. 'That's fine. I'm fourteen, so . . .'

But, anyway, like I said, we survived.

A man with a baseball cap and a huge grin helped me pull my pink suitcase out of the overhead locker. I felt awkward and when I thanked him he said, 'You're welcome, Princess.'

(I'd never been called *that* before.)

After we landed in Chicago, without crashing, I switched to school trip mode. The phone-checking, elbow-pumping crowd guided me to where I needed to go. Even though I'd been in the air for eight hours, the time difference meant it was still early morning. I gripped a dozen scraps of folded paper, all with the same details of the connecting flight: BA 1058, leaving from Gate H15 in Terminal 3.

And I didn't drop them once.

Not even when pulling my phone out to WhatsApp the family group chat.

I'm safe. It's snowy.

Dad was first to reply.

What's America like? You missed the connecting fight yet?

Ignoring the spelling mistake, I looked around.

Bit like England, I replied. *Smells weird. Connecting flight not left yet.*

Glove you so much. Can't believe you're there on your gown, messaged Mum. *Remember my glasses. Promise to stay safe.*

I didn't know what she meant about 'glasses' but guessed she was hitting the 'g' key when she didn't mean to. Autocorrect did the rest. Classic Mum.

Promise, I replied.

Flights over land get NIGHTMARE turbulence, messaged Amy.

She shouldn't be allowed to be a member of the group. She should be expelled from the family. I'd make this point when I got back home.

I walked a long corridor. At its end a genuine American police officer took my passport and travel forms. From under a heavy moustache and behind a Perspex screen, he asked why I was visiting the States and where my parents were. His voice sounded like a dog's bark. An angry dog. A dog that chases children around playgrounds.

'I've won a competition to be in a superhero film and my parents are in England.' He glanced up from his tiny battered computer screen. I'd caught his focus. And you don't want to be catching the focus of American cops at passport control. Airport rule number one. 'Movie.' I cleared my throat. 'My parents are probably asleep. The time difference. I don't know. Dad sometimes stays up late, eating cheese sandwiches and watching violent films. Or is it morning there?'

(When I get nervous I talk too much.)

'Are you trying to be funny, sir?'

First 'princess', now 'sir'. But the novelty was over-shadowed by the 100 per cent American cop stare focused my way. I'd seen this look in films. It wasn't one that led to something nice like being given a puppy or a burger.

'No, sir,' I said, and it was all I *could* say.

He got me to put my fingers on some kind of scanner. He swivelled something like a webcam and told me to look into it. Did this happen to everyone? Or was I a suspected criminal?

'Which superhero?' he asked.

'Sorry?'

'Which superhero movie?'

'They won't tell me.'

The cop stared a bit longer, and then stamped my passport.

'You want to know the best superhero to come out of Chicago?' Was he testing me? Before a word could emerge, my brain shrinking to a walnut, the man answered. 'Ghost Rider. You get yourself down to Kids on the Fly, you might have a pleasant surprise. You hear me?' I nodded. I did hear him. I just didn't understand him . . . He slid my passport back through the gap in the plastic. 'Nice luggage, by the way.'

Kids on the Fly? What did that mean?

I pulled the Princess past (regular, English) arrows pointing to the part of the airport with all the shops and restaurants. And when I arrived I let out a long breath. Bright lights and dull travellers surrounded me and my breathing. I was almost there.

Go, Jacob! You can do this! PMA!

Good news: the LA flight was listed on the big screen, even if some later ones had been cancelled 'due to adverse weather'.

Bad news: I had half an hour to kill before the gate even opened.

But there! A signpost! And one of the arms had 'Kids on the Fly' written on it. Wasn't that *exactly* what the police officer had said? Hadn't he also said that I'd have a nice surprise, and, like, immediately after he'd been talking about Ghost Rider, who is, actually, a sick superhero – don't let the movies fool you.

I walked past huge 4K TVs flashing feeds of worried weathermen and whirling storm graphics. Past travellers wearing the thick coats and the concerned faces of Arctic explorers. And every time I began to worry that maybe I'd missed 'Kids on the Fly', there came another sign with another arrow.

Maybe there'd be some graphic novels or a place to buy a baseball cap with 'Ghost Rider' written on it or some Metropolis candy or . . .

By now half an hour had gone: the gate was opening. If the place wasn't round the next corner, I decided, I'd turn back or else I might as well carry on walking all the way to LA. Giving up was the correct decision, the adult choice.

(Like an idiot, I carried on walking.)

CHAPTER 3

Nicolas Cage

'Kids on the Fly' was a soft-play area. A man who looked like he'd be more at home in a wrestling ring rose from a stool. He held up a hand and told me that I was too old by about ten years and he sat back down.

Behind him happy toddlers rolled around in a paddling pool filled with plastic balls.

'Hi. Yes. But I was told there was something to do with superheroes here, please?'

My voice had never sounded so small. The man stared at me. Maybe staring was more of a thing in the US. There *is* a lot of staring in American films and TV shows. Think about it.

Slowly he rotated his body, his bum squeaking against the plastic stool, a noise that in any other situation would have me sniggering into my hand. He pointed at the wall.

For a second I thought he wanted me to read the fire evacuation procedures. Then I realised he was indicating the signed picture of Nicolas Cage that hung next to them.

'Signed,' he said.

'That's fantastic,' I replied. 'So sick.'

It wasn't fantastic or sick. It was a signed picture of Nicolas Cage. He'd played Ghost Rider in two movies. He wasn't even dressed as the character in this picture. It was his face.

'I mean . . .' said the man.

'Yes,' I said. 'Really. Thank you.'

The stool man squinted at me like he suspected I was being sarcastic, which is more Amy's deal.

Back the way I'd come, a black screen of doom was flashing the warning 'final call' against the LA flight all of a sudden. Nooooooo. Pulling the Princess behind me, I sprinted for it.

It was at this moment that I first thought I might miss my connection. It didn't feel great, to be honest. Dad's last words haunted me. He'd been fairly clear about his preference concerning me catching the plane.

A glance at another passing screen now told me that the gate was closing. They must have been rushing the boarding process because of the snow.

I was *so* near. I was past all the shops and restaurants. I was in departures proper. People gripping boarding cards queued hopefully in roped-off areas. Huge windows showed tiny vehicles down below scraping the ever-falling snow off everything. There were planes outside. Big ones. Lined up, waiting for something, waiting for me.

My muscles stung, my breathing choked, but the finishing line was in sight – I experienced that final burst of adrenalin you get when the end of double PE is close.

I was the Flash, travelling so fast that I was invisible.

What gate's that? A square sign stuck out from the wall saying TWO. *Push on. I'm already passing* THREE. *Round the corner will be* FOUR. *I can do this! Jacob FTW!*

A crackling Tannoy announced the cancellation of a flight to Boston. Another message came immediately after – a flight to Seattle was off too. Had I missed an announcement? Had they called my name? I thought they were meant to call your name?

I needed to get to Gate Fifteen. I was at Five. The angles of the pentagonal corridor meant I couldn't see round the corner, obviously, but I knew my numbers.

I've always been good at maths. I was headed in the right direction, whether I made it or not was a question of time. So I upped the pace.

And I reckon I was operating at full running capacity.

I turned in the direction of Gate Fifteen. My throat was hot and sore. My heart beat in my ears. The corridor had emptied a little. Maybe everyone who'd needed to get on a plane had got on a plane.

Apart from me.

At Gate Fifteen there was nobody and nothing. I could see this all the way from Gate Eleven. But even if there *had* been a scrum of travellers, I kind of knew I'd be disappointed. Spidey-senses. The whole experience had been leading up to it. A huge American prank at my expense.

It was Dad's fault. This was *always* going to happen from the moment he'd warned me not to miss the flight. Some things are fated.

Gate Fifteen: plastic seats screwed to the ground. And a desk. And behind the desk a pair of grey doors. Closed. The only sign of human activity was an abandoned empty water bottle lying on its side.

A whispered 'no' escaped my mouth.

There were windows too. And through the windows

there was a huge plane. And snow fell over the huge plane and I felt like I might throw up. Because this was *my* huge plane. And *my* huge plane was taxiing through drifting snowflakes and away from the terminal and away from me. Inside, there would be a single empty seat. My empty seat.

I'd missed the connecting flight.

I was stuck in Chicago.

And it was because of Nicolas Cage.

Dad was going to go crazy.

CHAPTER 4

Proactive Man

Two hours later, I was freezing my everything off standing in a queue outside a bus station in downtown Chicago. The cold wasn't the worst thing: I had this acidic feeling that I'd made a galactic mistake in leaving the airport. The kind of mistake that couldn't be measured in being grounded.

There'd been a queue at BA customer services, the departure screens overflowing with red warnings of cancelled journeys. A voice said there would be no flights for twenty-four hours and all affected BA passengers would be put up in a hotel. The queue grumbled.

'Are you kidding me?' said a man with a massive beard.

I'd grab a burger. That's what I'd do. As soon as my accommodation was sorted. America. They do things differently here. I mean that was already obvious. The toilet stall doors didn't reach the floor for one thing.

It'll be fiiine. Dad doesn't even have to know, I told myself.

Eventually I got to the front of the airport queue and arrangements were arranged.

Maybe if, walking away from the desk, I hadn't looked up, I wouldn't have seen the huge sign saying TRANSPORTATION SOLUTIONS. But I did. I couldn't check into my hotel for ages, so I joined another queue of moaning people, those waiting for solutions to their transportation problems, and I wondered whether I should call home.

Thoughts:

If I go to the Holiday Inn, I'll sit in a tiny room until Snowmageddon ends. When I finally get to Hollywood I'll have missed my scene and all I'll have left to do is to jump back on a return flight home.

Or . . .

I could be PROACTIVE like . . .

PROACTIVE MAN. CAPTAIN PROACTIVE. THE PROACTIVATOR.

'How much is a train to LA?' I asked in my most self-assured voice, which didn't sound too self-assured if I'm honest.

The transportation solutions woman wore a smile as fake as her fingernails.

'Two hundred and eighty-five dollars.'

Right. I had a hundred.

'Is there a bus?'

I heard a long sigh from the American woman queuing behind me.

'There's the Greyhound. That'd get you there. Express route. You wouldn't even have to change. The roads are fine. It's eighty-five dollars. And you'll need another five to take the CTA to the bus station. Greyhound don't leave from here.'

I handed over the hundred-dollar bill. It didn't feel great. Especially as Mum was likely at some point to ask what I'd spent her money on.

'How old are you, honey? You've got to be fifteen to travel unaccompanied.'

I cleared my throat. I'd never lied to a proper official before. Only once when I told a gardener that it wasn't me who'd run across his lawn. And this official was American. What if she asked to see my passport? What if I got thrown in jail? American jail. With gangs and tattoos and orange jumpsuits.

'Sixteen,' I said. 'And British.'

(Only half was untrue. A 50 per cent lie. Not even a full fib.)

And that was that. She didn't even look up. She took my money. As I watched her quick fingernails I tried not to chunder. Because, as I told my stomach, I was sixteen in lots of ways. I mean, there were so going to be sixteen-year-olds less grown-up than me. For example, my legs were decently hairy.

'How long does it take to get to California?' I asked all innocently, which maybe I should have done before handing over the cash.

'Two days,' she said, slipping my money into an out-of-sight till and passing me ten dollars back. 'You arrive at nine ten in the morning on Thursday. Sometimes they even arrive ahead of schedule. You'll need to show photo ID and proof of age to your driver. Have a great journey.'

Two days! A double tap of bad news to the head. And on a bus too! There'd better be a socket for my phone.

Don't cry, don't cry.

Think: the schedule said that the scene was being shot midday on Thursday. Today was meant to be arrival and 'settling in'. For tomorrow, Wednesday, the plan was shopping in Beverly Hills. And, I mean, I didn't even like shopping. Or hills.

Thursday: they'd be able to pick me up from the Greyhound station in LA in the morning and get me to the studio in time. Easily. And I'd still have the studio tour to look forward to later on in the afternoon. It was fine. Really.

To try to ignore the weird turning of my insides, I remembered that time in Year Nine when Sean Williams was on TV. Bristol City were playing in the FA Cup and the camera showed the crowd. There he was. Looking moist in a bobble hat. But then the head teacher mentioned it in assembly. Sean's picture was in the newsletter. Sixth-form girls spoke to him. For real. Imagine that. The dream.

What would happen when they saw me in a movie? It'd be on the school website and everything. Forget top grades or goals scored – I'd be a hero. I'd have an entourage, and I could pick out my table in the school canteen and they'd let me skip the queue and never again would I worry about detentions because of late homework. Even Amy would be obliged to acknowledge my awesomeness. I'd get a cool nickname like 'Famous Jacob'. 'FJ'. 'Facob'. I mean, at the very least people would know my name.

The proof of age thing *was* a problem. But if the driver

didn't let me on the bus, I could just go back to the hotel, safe in the knowledge that at least I'd tried. And the weather would have to clear at some point. That's what weather does. Unless you're in northern England.

When I thanked the woman for the tickets her mouth said 'you're welcome' and 'have a nice day', but her eyes said 'not long until the end of my shift'.

Questions?

After taking a 'Blue Line' CTA train to a place called Clinton, I walked for ten minutes through real American streets with real American snow piled high. At some point an American must have gone crazy with a shovel around here. American cars splattered sleet on passing pedestrians, more coat than people, who swore, and nobody paid me any attention, which was great.

(That's a lie – some dude on a bike shouted, 'Nice suitcase.')

I finally arrived at the bus station. A man with an afro stood behind a desk.

'I'm John? How can I help you?'

Everything he said sounded like a question, which made our conversation really confusing.

'Is this the right place for a bus to Los Angeles, please?'

'Buses all over the country from here, sir?'

Was that a yes or no? Before I could work out how best to ask again, he continued. 'You want a ticket to LA? How old are you? I can't be selling any tickets without proof of age or an unaccompanied minors form?'

'I've got the ticket already,' I said, struggling to pull it from my coat pocket. 'I'm sixteen and British. Thanking you.'

John stared.

'I don't want to see the ticket? I thought you looked young, that's all? No problem? The LA service leaves at 11.05? That's just over one hour's time? Boarding begins twenty minutes before the departure? Tie this round your suitcase handle and hold on to the receipt? Hand your luggage to the driver on boarding? I've always wanted to see London? Is it super sweet?'

I nodded. I thought this was the safest tactic.

The waiting room was empty. A TV played in the corner, warning of 'severe weather' and 'unprecedented disruption'. My phone's battery was already down to 27 per cent because why wouldn't it be? I messaged Mum.

Problem with plane but now on bus, so everything's okay! LOL.

(I couldn't contact Marvel because I didn't have their number. The only arrangement made was a promise of someone at LAX holding a sign with my name on it.)

Three seconds later, my phone started vibrating. Mum. And she didn't even say 'hi'.

'What do you mean there was a problem with the plane? Where are you?' I could hear rumbling in the background. It wasn't thunder; it was worse – it was Dad. 'Your father wants to know if you missed the connection.'

'I'm on a bus. Like when we went to Bath for that wedding but the train was cancelled. It's fine,' I said.

There was a rustling sound like Mum had dropped the phone in a bucket of leaves. (I don't think she had.)

Dad's voice barked from the other end. 'Did you miss the connection, Jacob? Tell me the truth. Don't lie to your father.'

'There aren't any planes flying,' I replied, which was a clever response because it was true. 'It's very snowy here but everything's fine. I'm on a bus and I'll be in Hollywood soon. I'd better go because I haven't got much battery left.'

'Stay safe,' commanded Dad. 'And don't go leaving the bus. Not even for the toilet.'

Before saying goodbye, Mum made me promise to keep hydrated, which was contradicting Dad if you think about it.

I turned the phone off. Parents: my Kryptonite. I sat and tried to think about the movie to make myself feel better. Visualisation. Maybe this (sitting in a downtown bus station) was what it was like to be an extra? I tried imagining being on set, of being introduced to genuine Hollywood actors, but my thoughts always returned to the conversation with home. My lies hung over me like a snow cloud.

The front doors snapped open and a girl, who looked old enough to drive, ran through to John's desk. A ponytail of dark braids flashed from a blue baseball cap and across her shoulders. She moved like she was training for a marathon and couldn't stop because it would ruin the workout. But this wasn't the weirdest thing – she held a box wrapped in brown paper. I say 'held' but she was more hugging it. It was the perfect shape to contain a football, although that probably wasn't what she had in there because Americans, like Dad, don't 'get' soccer.

I pretended to scratch my neck and turned to watch. She was all energy, her muscles jerking. She asked for a single on the first bus to Los Angeles. There was something about her face that suggested you'd not want to upset her. Or, at least, that she wanted you to think that you'd not want to upset her.

'How old are you, miss?' asked John. 'Minors need a letter—'

She interrupted him. 'Seventeen. Here's my ID.'

She paid. Her ticket cost less than mine but there was no way I was ever going to complain. She asked where the restroom was and disappeared in its direction. She was either really nervous or really confident. I stopped thinking about her (after ten minutes) to return to worrying about being sat alone in a Chicago bus station.

Soon, but not massively, a big blue coach pulled up outside, its engine shaking the ground. It was like one you might take for school trips, the type where we'd all pile on to the back seats before the teachers could stop us.

'There's your coach, sir?' said John.

'Is it?' I asked.

'It is?'

I saw LOS ANGELES above the driver's window, so decided that John wasn't asking me a question but stating a fact. I stood up. I turned the Princess on to her wheels and stepped towards the exit. I checked my pockets for my wallet and my phone. Neither was there. Both objects lay on the chair where I'd been sitting.

I stepped silently to grab them. The Princess toppled over, like she was jetlagged and had fallen asleep. There was a bang from the direction of the restroom and out came the girl, running and saying, 'This my ride?'

And I would have warned her about the resting Princess, ankle-high and pink, but she moved too quickly. The parcel she held must have obscured her view or something. Her feet struck the bag and she tripped, flying through the air and crunching her face and arms against the front doors, which stood unopened and impassive. Her parcel, a perfect cube in brown paper, bounced away like a die.

'Ugh,' I said, my brain glitching. This wasn't good.

She yelped. And the noise crackled through the space.

'Are you okay, ma'am?' asked John, standing and definitely asking a question.

Frozen at the chair, holding my wallet and phone, I hated the snow and especially hated Marvel, but only briefly, for not putting me on a direct flight.

'Whose pink bag is this?' she asked, standing up and cradling her wrist and, somehow, grabbing her box like a squirrel finding the last acorn of autumn.

At least she hadn't died, I thought as I raised a hand. 'Sorry?' I said.

(The whole question thing was contagious.)

'You've broken my arm. Open the door for me. I mean...'

She glared/winced as I did what I was told. Cold air rushed in like it needed the toilet. John asked if she required first aid, but she ignored him.

'Great job, Princess,' she said, stepping out, leaving John and me gawping from the waiting room.

'You think she's okay?' he asked. 'She really slammed into those doors?'

'I hope so?' I replied. 'I don't know?'

Because I didn't. Not about her and not about anything.

'Hey, I like your bag, though,' said John. 'Is that a Brit thing?'

Girl Trouble

There was a sudden queue: all moaning desperation to get on the coach, all stomping sneakers in the slush, all saying, 'We're freezing here.' Most looked alone and in their twenties or thirties – old. There was also a dog running about, snapping at snowflakes. I watched him for a while and briefly forgot everything but, in particular, my need for photo ID . . . and the broken girl.

And, as my grandad used to say, it was colder than the hinges of hell.

'If you've got a luggage receipt, your luggage is going in. If you don't, you need one and not from me. Understand, yo?' said the driver. In return came shouting and barking. 'And somebody needs to shut that mutt up.'

The queue shrank as the bus filled, but there was a

growing stack of bags piled on the sidewalk like a local luggage shop had exploded.

The driver's mouth blew tiny clouds as he spoke, reminding me of the cold.

'Ticket and ID, please.' I handed over my ticket and passport. 'Is this your bag?' he said, nodding towards the Princess but not looking up from my documents.

'I've a baggage receipt,' I said and he nodded, focusing on the passport page with my photo, my name and my date of birth.

'Thank you.'

Would he have noticed my age if the dog, which had spent the last fifteen minutes barking, hadn't cocked its leg against the luggage? I don't know.

'Come on!' he shouted. 'Whose dog *is* that? John! John! Give me a hand, John! There's a dog dirtying the baggage again, man.'

The driver shoved my ticket and passport into my chest and went for the dog.

Standing at the very front of the coach, I couldn't see any spare seats. Everybody had their heads bowed, immersed in phones. I walked the line. The forest of heads thinned out. I could see a free window seat. *And* I could also see who I'd be sitting next to.

I mean . . . there were literally no other free seats. It didn't matter. So I ignored the fluttering in my chest. Because it wasn't like I was *choosing* to sit next to her.

Her arms rested on top of that same parcel that had gone tumbling in the waiting room. She cradled her right wrist, the fingers of her left gently kneading its skin. (Guilt klaxon.) Her neck was sharply angled and she stared out of the window. She bit into her bottom lip. This was the same girl who'd stormed into the waiting area but with all the worry turned up.

'Excuse me,' I said, voice as steady as jelly, like I'd never talked to a girl before, which I had. 'Sorry, but is this seat free?'

'You've got to be kidding me,' she said.

After I'd managed to cram my coat into an overhead locker, she'd swung her legs to the side, expending the minimum effort required to let me pass. I'd excused myself and sat down so very quietly.

'I think you've broken my wrist, by the way,' she said, sending waves of resentment from her eyes to my face. 'Like for real. I'm crippled for life.'

'Do you want me to ask the driver if there's any wrist medicine?'

This was a fair request, even if it made me sound like a primary-school kid.

'Do you want me to ask the driver if there's any wrist medicine?' she repeated, putting on the lamest British accent you could imagine. 'What's wrist medicine?'

She also relaxed all the muscles in her face and rolled her eyes into their sockets, making like she thought I was an idiot, which I'm not.

I turned to look at the snow. It was, like, at least five times warmer than my neighbour.

Was it snowing back in England? Was it snowing outside my bedroom window? On to next door's black Citroën? Had Mum and Dad got back from work? Was Amy getting told off for having her earphones in? It was like knowing a film you loved was playing without you in a distant cinema. Life went on back home, in those familiar patterns, because that's what life does. I guess, in that way, being on holiday was like being dead. Everyone makes a fuss about it but ultimately it's boring.

'Are you for real?' she asked. 'I'm not joking. Are you? For real?'

'Yes,' I said, not meeting her eyes but also not wanting

to be hassled for the whole journey. 'I am for real. One hundred per cent real, that's me.'

'That accent! I mean.'

I nodded, even though it wasn't me with an accent – it was her.

She'd tripped over *my* bag – okay – but if she refused to get her wrist looked at, that wasn't *my* fault. And, anyway, it wasn't as if there was bone breaking skin or blood pumping out.

(If only she could regenerate – that's got to be the best superpower; you'd be invincible. Any wound: instantly healed. People talk about choosing between flying and invisibility but, for me, being able to heal wounds is up there. Check out Wolverine and Deadpool.)

As soon as the bus chugged out of Chicago's suburbs there wasn't much to look at. There were USB ports for phones between the two seats in front of us and that was something, at least. Although . . . my cable was buried in the Princess and I didn't get the feeling that the driver would be too keen to go rooting through the luggage compartment.

There was one weird moment, which made sense later, and it happened at a traffic light. The bus had pulled up to a red. Alongside us a black pick-up truck rolled to a stop. There was no snow on the vehicle at all, like its metal was sending out heatwaves that melted flakes before they could settle.

The driver's window descended and a man with an enormous white moustache looked up – not at the bus, but at me. He locked my eyes in a stare that was only broken when the lights changed and the bus started forward. For some reason I shuddered.

Americans sure are weird, I thought.

At some point I must have dozed off. Because, later, I definitely woke up and when I did there were three massive shocks:

1. The bus wasn't moving.
2. Two police officers stood at the front. One had a microphone and the other held an iPad, its screen facing forward.
3. The girl's head rested against my shoulder. Still wearing that baseball cap, bright blue with an orange C above the brim.

I didn't move. Not a muscle of a muscle. A bit because of the police but mainly: the girl. What would she say if

I woke her? Had I ever had one fall asleep on me before? A girl?

I didn't know. But what I *did* know were all the feelings sparked off by the experience. Mad and confusing. Like a talking horse. My mind was a muddled soup of fear and longing. It could only be straightened out through getting back to sleep. Which was kind of a problem in the current situation.

Her head was warm. I could feel it through my top. And even though she was sleeping, she still gripped that box. It must contain something pretty valuable like . . . silver coins, for instance, or a really expensive puppy (cryogenically frozen).

'Thank you for your time, ladies and gentlemen. We won't hold you for long. We're stopping all buses going through the Champaign region on account of reports of a dangerous runaway minor. My colleague is holding an iPad with a recent image of the suspect. We would ask that you study this as we walk the aisle. Please raise your hand if you recognise the individual or if you have any questions. Thank you for your attention.'

The microphone squawked as he handed it back to the driver. A burst of rock music shook through the coach before the driver managed to turn it off. Both officers made to walk forward at the same time. Their shoulders banged and there was a split second of awkwardness, which didn't help create an appearance of professionalism.

To begin with I was confused by the word 'minor'. I'd thought, you see, that he'd meant 'miner' and imagined some tiny guy with a hard hat and pickaxe running about. As soon as I saw the iPad's picture, though, I understood my mistake.

Because it was so her. The girl *was* the girl, if you know what I mean. The girl with her head on my shoulder. Wanted by the police and everything. She probably had stolen gold in the box. Or, like, rare butterflies. I don't know.

What should I do? There was that time in Chemistry when Al Philips held Emma Ashton's pencil case over the Bunsen burner and even though I saw, I never told Dr Adiga. The whole class were put in a lunchtime detention and Emma's parents came into school to see the deputy head the next day.

I'd had anxiety dreams about that situation for, like, months afterwards. And we're talking about Dr Adiga, who everyone joked wore glasses because he couldn't control his pupils. Not two American police officers with belts that contained all kinds of devices meant to hurt and control you, not forgetting their actual guns.

What *had* she done? When I'd seen her back at the station the first thing I'd thought was how tense she looked. Like the way she gritted her teeth. On edge. Focused like a criminal.

I'd definitely never had a criminal fall asleep on me before. I'd have thought it would be less comfortable.

CHAPTER 7

Bad Memes
Champaign, Illinois

I could literally feel my intestines tighten as the police approached. I'd seen enough American movies and TV shows to know what happened to snitches.

Stitches.

But, really, I should put my hand up. And right now. Why cover for a stranger? The police called her 'dangerous'. That doesn't sound good. That sounds painful.

(But could a monster feel this warm?)

Should I wake her? Let her deal with it? I don't even know her name. Look, what's in the parcel? No writing. No address. No stamps. Just brown wrapping paper. Drugs? Money? Someone's head? Oh my days, an actual head. Maybe a cat's head? There's someone killing cats near Bristol. Mum had said. Maybe she's a cat killer. Maybe she has a dead cat in her box? Or a live cat? Or a stolen cat? Or loads of kittens?

No, this is getting silly. She'd not be in trouble for carrying a cat around. It's definitely drugs. They're mad for them in America. Maybe if I excuse myself to go to the toilet and lock the cubicle until everything's done, that would be okay? I'd show my passport.

'I got confused,' I'd say. 'I'm British and on my way to Hollywood.'

Thinking about the box's contents didn't help. I needed to control my breathing: in through the nose and out through the mouth. Or was it the other way? I didn't know! And why hadn't I put my hand up yet?! Was my breathing suspicious-looking?

I let out a tiny fart. Luckily it was silent.

Where was the responsible adult to tell me what to do? There should be an app. You'd type in your problem and a teacher would reply with the correct decision. Only, I *knew* the right thing to do – I should tell the police. I should be a good citizen. If they wanted her, she'd have done something bad, right? That's how it works.

One officer moved up the aisle with the other close behind. It was like the dinner service on the flight over, which was something that felt a lifetime ago. The female cop showed both sides of seats the iPad and all the passengers shook their heads. If someone else had seen her, that would save me a decision. But they'd all been on their phones when we'd got on.

(Meaning maybe all the teachers/parents have been right all along? Phones *are* bad for society. It didn't stop *them* using the things, though.)

'Hey,' I hissed at the baseball cap in such a way that if you were looking at me, either in real time or a later CCTV recording, you'd not see my lips moving. 'Hey!'

But my sleeping neighbour didn't stir, and the police were now only six rows away.

'Do you have any trail mix, ma'am?' an elderly passenger asked the cops and I had no idea what she meant.

But there *was* hope, I realised, and that hope was the hat. It was pulled so far down over the girl's face that, because she was turned to me, there'd be no recognising her from the aisle.

I would stay silent. Result. Best decision ever. Because it wasn't a decision. And I wouldn't be betraying her or lying to the police. Because I didn't have it in me to deceive officials twice in one day. And these two were proper cops. With the faces and everything. I mean, the girl on the iPad wasn't wearing a baseball cap, so . . .

There was a split second of panic as I wondered what Dad would say if he knew what was happening to his son (me) at this precise moment (are parents telepathic?) and also the decisions made to get here. But it was because of me that she'd hurt her wrist and not grassing her up to the police would kind of mean we were quits, right? It made sense.

The female cop was actually leaning across the girl and into me and showing me the iPad. Its screen was bright and hurt my eyes. Cruel and unusual punishment. The image was something you might see on social media. The girl was smiling but also wincing like the sun was in her eyes.

At the bottom of the picture was a single word.

MISSING.

It looked like a meme gone bad.

'Is this individual with you?' asked the female cop, pointing down to the girl. 'This individual with the . . . package?'

This wasn't fair. I hadn't been expecting an out-and-out question. My throat felt all pink and tiny.

'I'm sorry,' I just about said.

'I didn't catch that,' said the male cop.

'I'm sorry,' I said.

'Are you from around here, sir?' asked the male cop, speaking loud and slow.

The way that police ask questions makes you feel guilty. Something in the tone. Maybe it's part of their training. And this here now at this moment was how all bad stuff started. I could feel it, the world's tightening focus and also the bad stuff. I struggled for control of my thoughts and voice.

'I'll be the one asking questions,' said the female cop. 'Are you from around here, son?'

One deep breath. Through the nose. And relax.

'No,' I said. 'I'm British. And I'm heading for Los Angeles to be in a superhero movie because I won a competition. I was supposed to be on a plane but I missed it and then there weren't any other planes because of the snow but my attitude is that if I keep my head down and stay out of trouble but stay *on* the bus, it won't make a huge amount of difference, so . . .'

They stared open-mouthed. Eventually the woman spoke.

'Are you trying to be funny, sir?'

Why do all the police think that? I'm only a kid from Somerset trying to get to Hollywood without upsetting anyone.

'No.'

I shook my head and felt tears spiking behind my eyes. I should just confess all! Let them arrest me!

Take me away, officers! It's a fair cop! Yes! It's her! She's the one you want!

'Are we going to be moving any time soon or are we going to be moving any time soon? I've got me a dying grandmother to get to,' shouted a gruff voice from the front of the bus. 'And the Lord sure ain't waiting!'

'Is this individual with you?' asked the female cop again, nodding to the girl.

'Yes,' I replied. 'She's British too.'

The cop stared as if she could look into my mind. And if she could, she'd have seen a tornado of confusion. Like, obviously the girl wasn't British; she was wearing a baseball cap for one thing.

The police officer put a palm to her partner's back and pushed him on.

'Stay out of trouble,' he said, as he stepped to the next line of passengers. 'They don't like strangers around these parts.'

I don't think I breathed again until they'd left the bus and the deep thud of its engine started, sending vibrations throughout the cabin like the crazy nerves shaking my body.

And, through it all, the girl stayed asleep.

CHAPTER 8

Saucy Boy
St Louis, Missouri

We stopped in a place called St Louis, which is pronounced SAINT LEWIS. Snow dusted cars and sidewalks, but it wasn't as deep as Chicago.

The driver announced that we'd have an hour to eat, if we wanted, in the 'food court' inside the St Louis Greyhound station. There were empty seats dotted about the bus now – there must have been stops I'd slept through. And even though it wasn't even six yet, most remaining passengers were out cold, including the girl. She no longer had her head resting against my shoulder, which meant I could go.

I hadn't moved so quietly and carefully since creeping downstairs last Christmas morning to squeeze presents. First off, I stood up, my chest pushing against the back of the chair ahead and my head bowed but still scraping against the plastic underside of the overhead lockers. I pulled one leg up, like a spider ballerina, and then placed it delicately between the girl's.

Although I didn't touch her, and made no noise whatsoever – even my jeans were silent – she stirred. I froze, waiting until she returned to regular breathing. This wasn't a great position to be caught in.

A woman walked down the aisle, stopping to turn and look at me and shake her head like I was another example of the state of kids today.

I lifted my other leg and managed to swing it all the way over the girl's lap and into the aisle. Turning, my backside was now dangerously close to her face. For a second of panic I thought I might overbalance, meaning I'd end up sitting on the girl. My life would be as good as over. I managed to grip a plastic handle on a chair across the aisle and saved myself.

I stood like a stretching dancer, my left arm and right leg forming a perfectly straight line. Was that a bead of sweat running down my forehead? All I needed to do was pull my right leg from her lap and I was free.

'Kindly get your ass out of my face,' said the girl, not moving.

I half hopped, half fell and ended up lying face down in the aisle. I apologised and said I hadn't wanted to wake her.

'I wasn't asleep,' she said, her voice coming from the darkness under the brim of her cap. 'What's going down? Apart from you.'

'We've stopped for food. I was going to stretch my legs. Sorry.'

'Get me a Happy Meal. Chicken nuggets. BBQ sauce.'

'I haven't really got . . .'

Her left hand flicked up. Between her fingers was a twenty-dollar note folded once lengthways.

'Take it,' she said. 'Get yourself something. But don't forget the BBQ sauce. I love BBQ sauce more than life.'

I took the money, even though it was probably criminal. Her hand returned to the package. She asked what I was waiting for.

I'm not sure I've ever been so hungry as I was in the queue for McDonald's. The 'food court' was like one you'd find in service stations off UK motorways: really expensive tiny versions of fast-food chains, the smell of fat hanging in the air like drops of grease in water.

I turned on my phone to check for messages. Nothing came through. Its battery had been at 27 per cent when

I'd last checked. It was now at 15 per cent. *And* it had been switched off.

Maybe batteries deplete faster in America? Because of the foreign electricity? No, that doesn't work.

After eating, I'd ask the driver if I could get my charger out of the Princess. I mean, that was an entirely reasonable request. No reason for him to think me an idiot or anything.

When my food came, I took it to a free table. Our RS teacher often said we should take joy in the moment. As I unwrapped my cheeseburger, I finally understood what she meant.

Don't worry about being in a place called Missouri, a word you can't spell, let alone find on a map. Don't worry about the girl and the police. Don't worry about Mum or Dad. Consider only the cheeseburger: the true meaning of life.

And as I opened my mouth to take a bite . . .

'You get my BBQ sauce?'

She stood before me. If she'd not been holding her package, she'd have had her hands on her hips for sure.

Yeah, so I'd forgotten the sauce, and there was sighing and eye-rolling and I thought I was about to be sassed to death. Sassocuted.

'If I give you this package, do you swear to God that

you won't lose it or drop it or whatever other lame British stuff you might do because you're lame?'

I nodded, my mouth full of cheeseburger. She handed over the package. As she did so, I could see a faint bruise that circled her right wrist like a friendship bracelet. It didn't look *that* bad. I mean, I'd prefer she hadn't fallen over the Princess, but . . . it obviously wasn't broken.

She saw where I was looking.

'It still hurts,' she said. 'Like hell. I can't even be driving myself anywhere now.'

'Sorry.'

The box was heavier than you'd imagine. It was weighty enough to be a pain to carry everywhere. Especially if you'd hurt your arm. I shook it very gently. Did it rattle? I wasn't sure. Why hadn't she left it on the bus? It must contain something massively valuable. Drugs, cash, diamonds. Gulp.

She was soon back with the sauce. And she was quick to recover the package, placing it between her and her food, which meant she had to eat round it.

When finished, she wiped her mouth with a serviette and stared.

'My name's Jennifer. Not Jenny. Not Jen. But Jennifer. Don't forget that.'

'Jennifer,' I said. 'I won't forget.'

'Too right you won't. I'd shake your hand but it's covered in ketchup, which is totally disgusting. And it's all around your mouth. Also, you broke my wrist, so, you know, any movement is total agony.'

'I could get you some . . .'

'I've got Advil.'

I nodded like I understood. So was she going to tell me what was happening or . . .

'What's *your* name?' (She continued talking so I couldn't answer. She leant forward, hands on the package, voice lowered. She even glanced behind her to check nobody was listening.) 'Thanks for covering with the police. Appreciated. I thought it was over. You didn't have to do that. So I could almost forgive you. For breaking my wrist.' Her eyes narrowed. 'Almost.'

'I'm Jacob,' I said. 'And all this is pretty new to me.'

Nervous laugh.

'Same.'

I asked *the* question.

'Yeah. So. Why are the police after you? I mean, you look too old to be in trouble for running away from home.' She didn't reply. 'So –' my mind raced through the other questions I wanted to ask – 'is it what's in the parcel? Is that why they're after you?'

She stood from the table. I guess we've all got secrets.

'I'm going to the bathroom,' she said. 'If you've never ridden Greyhound before, you should do the same. The on-board one gets gross. Where're you headed?'

'Hollywood.'

'No way. All the way to LA? For real? Are you going to be in a movie?'

'No but really. I am. I won a competition. I had to write a poem about my favourite superhero.' (Why did I tell her that?) 'But, you know, I'm not one of *those* kids.'

I sounded like a five-year-old. She raised a single eyebrow.

'What kids?'

'You know, the ones who think it's all real. Fantasyland. I don't think it's real. I don't camp overnight to get tickets for the release of the new Avengers movie.'

(Lie.)

'You like superhero stuff?' I looked to the tray, nodding with the shame of the bullied. 'That's lit.' I looked up. She wasn't even mocking me. 'I'm going to LA as well. It's warmer out there. People are friendlier. I mean, that's not true, but . . .'

'Sounds good,' I said.

'What's the poem?'

I felt an ice-chill travel through my body.

Never ask me about the poem. Especially never ask me to recite it.

'Nothing. I don't remember.'

She shrugged. 'Okay,' she said. 'Be like that.' She pointed at the package. 'I'm trusting you to babysit it. Don't let it out of your sight.'

She hesitated as if, in actual fact, she didn't trust me. But her bladder must have intervened and so she left, her braids bouncing as she went. 'Be like that,' she'd said. If there were anyone being anything, it was her.

She'd left a single fry. I popped it into my mouth, trying not to think about how *she* was travelling to LA, trying not to admit *why* I'd lied to the police, trying only to return to the sleepy, safe Jacob of sleepy, safe Somerset.

CHAPTER 9

The Cowboy

'Howdy.'

The voice came from nowhere, a man materialising from a cowboy film. He stood behind Jennifer's empty seat, thick fingers gripping the top of the chair. His skin was brown and wrinkled as if he'd spent his whole life burying bodies in the desert. He wore a black cowboy hat pushed slightly back from his forehead. He had a denim jacket buttoned to his chin, which made it look as if he were hiding secrets. And violent ones too.

He eyeballed the parcel. I edged it closer. His eyes followed. He didn't ask if the seat were free; he didn't repeat his 'howdy'. He just stood there.

I remembered the black pick-up I'd seen from the bus.

And this was *so* very much the same guy, the driver. Curling round his tight, thin lips was that dead caterpillar of a moustache. It belonged in the National History Museum.

I looked past his facial hair, to the door to the toilets, praying for Jennifer to return. She seemed like the type to know what to do when tall mute cowboys stood at your table without saying anything.

'I've finished my food,' I said, smiling like I was looking into the sun, because I had to say something.

'That I can see,' he said in as cowboy a voice as you could imagine, especially if you're from Somerset. 'Me? I've never had much time for French fries. I'm more of a grits man.'

I felt like I should offer him some food, but all that was left was a tiny fragment of lettuce. He didn't look like he'd enjoy tiny fragments of lettuce. I mean, he wasn't a rabbit.

'I like burgers,' I said, and I don't know why.

The Cowboy stared.

'You sound like you're a long way from home, son.'

And I think he would have continued staring if he hadn't started coughing. It was a hacking, rattling sound. And as his body bent in two, Jennifer appeared behind him. She froze outside the toilet door. Her face fell as she saw the Cowboy. She recognised him and you could see she wanted to run. But she was tied to that parcel, the one on my table, as securely as a dog to a lead. So, slowly pushing the door open behind her, she shook her head. She drew a line across her neck.

'Do you want some water?' I asked, shrugging my shoulders at Jennifer, as the Cowboy's lungs cracked the air. 'I could get some.'

Recovering, he noticed that I looked past his shoulder. He turned. But all there was to see was the closing toilet door. He pulled a handkerchief from his pocket and dabbed at his mouth.

'You here on your own, son?'

'I'm on holiday with my British family. We're British holidaymakers. From Britain.'

I don't think I'd ever said 'holidaymakers' before. It was a word my gran would use when trying to buy the *Daily Mail* from a Spanish newsagent's.

'Uh-huh?' said the Cowboy. 'Is that so? Where are your parents? If you called out, could they hear you?'

I smiled in a kind of dentist's-waiting-room way.

'They're in the toilets. Their stomachs.' I indicated the fast food restaurant. 'You know. British.'

His eyes fixed on the parcel. He moved to speak but thought better of it. Instead he smiled. You might have expected rotten teeth or ones coated in silver. But they were film-star perfect. How old *was* he? There was something treelike to him. Like you could work out his age by cutting him open and counting the rings.

'You're right. Excuse my . . . lack of manners. I'm no great conversationalist.' He touched the brim of his hat. 'You have yourself a swell time. Enjoy the bus journey. I'll be seeing you.'

Back on the coach, Jennifer didn't even let me ask the driver about my phone charger. She rushed me through to my seat with urgent, shaking hands.

'It's just that my phone's at, like, fourteen per cent.' Sitting now, Jennifer had her head in her hands, her elbows balanced on the parcel. Her legs trembled. I decided to stop talking about batteries. 'You okay?'

'What do *you* think?' she said.

'No? I mean, the guy was creepy. Maybe he was just really old. People get weird when they're old. My gran . . .'

My voice faded. I was doing it again: nervous talking. I turned to check if there were any free seats nearby. Maybe sitting somewhere else would be a good idea.

Jennifer raised her head. Her fingers picked at her nails.

'The *guy* works for my grandmother. A fixer. They call him the Cowboy. The police have failed, so now she's sent him.'

'The Cowboy? You knew him? Are they real?'

'Are what real?'

'Cowboys?'

Jennifer blinked at me.

'What are you talking about?'

I shook my head.

'Cowboys. I didn't realise they were a thing.'

'Look, there was this time a –' she did air quotation marks – '*business associate* of my grandmother's ran off with some money. Took a suitcase on a plane to Hawaii with a fake name, fake ID, everything. Who should be waiting for him as he steps out in Honolulu? The Cowboy. With the business associate's name on A4 laminated card and everything. You want to know what happened to the business associate?'

'They killed him?'

'Worse.'

I laughed. Jennifer didn't. I decided, like, maybe leaving this was a good idea.

'He wasn't expecting you,' she continued. 'He held off. But he's on our trail. It's only a matter of time now. He was a US marshal back in the day. He knows what he's doing. You're just a complication.'

'I've never been called that before.' Jennifer didn't react, not even with a half-grin. 'So what will you do?'

'I'll think of something. Don't sweat. He's not the problem. Grandmother is the problem.'

'Why?'

'You want to know why? I'll tell you why. You like superheroes – who's the bad guy from Superman?'

'Lex Luthor?'

'Yeah. That's the dude. Grandmother's him.'

'She's bald?'

'She'll be pissed at me running off. And taking this –' she patted the parcel –'will have turned her nuclear.'

I'd thought things were bad when I'd missed the flight. Now I'd covered for a girl wanted by the police and found out she was being pursued by some cowboy dude, *and* had stolen from her scary grandmother, who was also Lex Luthor.

My eyes pricked with hot tears. I turned away from Jennifer. I tried to clear my head. I tried to pretend that everything was okay and I was, like, on a bus to school or something.

'Did you say you had painkillers?' I said in a tissue-thin voice. 'I think my allergies are flaring up.'

CHAPTER 10

Emergency Exit

It was dark when I woke, shaken conscious by Jennifer's good hand. She was hissing swear words. The windows were so dark they may as well have been a painted backdrop. Night extended silently over fields forever.

We weren't moving, the engine was as dead as the view, but two figures up front were. Their dull outlines crept closer, illuminated by the odd spotlight of a passenger's phone. They weren't the police. Metal jangled. It was the driver and . . . the dark outline of a cowboy hat looming.

'Jennifer Lewis,' said the Cowboy. 'Time to come home.'

His voice sounded singsong. Like he was a primary-school teacher, not a mean man with a hat. Maybe he was trying to make Jennifer feel relaxed? Whatever the reason, she'd been right. His tracking skills were on point.

What happened next wasn't me being decisive. Or friendly. Or anything other than really tired. Jennifer dropped her parcel into my lap, its corners hurting my testicles a bit, and gripped my hand and whispered, 'You've *got* to help me. Please. Carry this.'

I tripped along behind Jennifer as she pulled me in her wake. The package was wedged against my chest, pinned there with my free arm. People slept on either side and only stirred when the Cowboy and the driver started shouting and drumming their feet up the aisle after us. We ran, Jennifer's baseball cap flying off her head, bouncing against my shoulder and dropping into the darkness behind.

Honestly, I didn't think we'd jump from the emergency exit at the rear of the bus . . . not until we actually did.

'Stop, kids!' called the Cowboy after us. 'You've nowhere to go!'

But he was wrong. The emergency exit cracked and whined as we fell through into the night. And we were instantly struck, not by a car – the coach had stopped in a lay-by – but by the sudden cold. It was like jumping into an Arctic lake. I guess.

'My coat,' I whimpered, but Jennifer was having none of it.

It was lucky that we'd tumbled into a ditch instead of a chasm or reservoir or alligator pit. But tumble we did, down and away from the bus's red and white rear lights.

Down here, the darkness was more silver than black. You could see the pencil outlines of everything. Somewhere, behind clouds, the moon shone. I tried to stop my teeth chattering – half nerves, half freezing.

'Jenny, honey, this ain't no game. Come home.'

The words echoed through the night like a gunshot. 'Home,' the Cowboy had said. And that made me think about Somerset and made me realise that it wasn't only the Princess and the coat on the bus but also my phone and wallet.

'Your English friend doesn't need all this,' he tried. 'Can you hear me, amigo? I'm here to help. Don't listen to Jenny's stories.'

And it was as if Jennifer could read my mind because as I was about to call out she, with two hands, wrist magically healed, covered my mouth and pulled me into a kind of hug that might have been sweet in different circumstances.

The Cowboy *would* find us out here in this ditch. All I had to do was nothing again. I wouldn't be snaking Jennifer and I wouldn't be committing to the obviously stupid action of staying with her. This cowboy man would let me get back on the bus and everything would be fine.

Just wait until his torchlight strikes.

Under a thousand white pinpricks we could hear everything – super-hearing – the scuffed boots of crocodile leather or snakeskin or whatever it is cowboys wear getting quieter as his shouts became more distant because . . . you wouldn't believe it but . . . he was heading the wrong way.

What'd happened to his immense tracking skills?

'Quit licking my hand,' whispered Jennifer.

I felt the words emerge from her chest before I heard them. She removed her fingers from my mouth.

'I wasn't,' I hissed back.

'You still got my package?'

I pushed it into her. She grunted. I'd lost all feeling in my nose. It was terrible.

'It's cold,' I said, my lips so frozen they felt like dead sausages.

I struggled to stand.

'Wait.'

Jennifer grabbed at my shirt and pulled me down. And in one . . . two . . . three . . . the bus's engine coughed into life.

Another voice, the driver's. He spoke about a schedule, about paying customers, and added, 'I saw them on the road. Heading towards Marshfield.'

The returning Cowboy grumbled an unhappy-sounding response as a hand found my collar. And it held my collar down. And I tried with all my strength to break free but it was like I was pinned by adamantine. I wasn't worrying about whispering now; I was worrying about being lost in the middle of the freezing nowhere. *And* without a coat. Mum would be doubly mad. Hypothermia. They get it on Duke of Edinburgh hikes.

'No,' I whined. 'Please. I'm not American. And my nose is *so* cold.'

The coach's headlights drew a crescent over us. Its engine purred into a higher gear, propelling the Greyhound to LA with all my stuff, including the hopes and the dreams, and without me.

My body trembled. I was about to shout, but the words caught in my throat as the Cowboy, still there in the darkness, spoke in a growl.

'I'm leaving, Jennifer. This is your final chance. Let's

not allow things to get unpleasant. You know I'll find you in the end.'

Her grip loosened, but I didn't break free. The Cowboy's words had paralysed me. They say there's a tiny part of your brain that hasn't evolved since we were lizards and it was that part, not my logical human brain, that froze my limbs, shut down my mouth.

Another engine fired up. Tyres coughed over stones. And so the Cowboy drove off and away, searching for our shadows in all the wrong places.

All I had left was my passport, still in the pocket where I'd shoved it back in Chicago, a useless Greyhound ticket, and a really heavy feeling about the epic-sized trouble I was now in.

CHAPTER 11

Kidnapped!
Somewhere near Springfield, Missouri

'You've kidnapped me,' I hissed in the ditch. 'So not cool.'

(Captain America was kidnapped once but that didn't make me feel any better.)

Why wasn't I shouting? There was nobody else around. The Cowboy and Greyhound had both gone. The distant growl of faraway engines was all the company we had.

Jennifer was already scrambling out of the ditch and heading for the road. And it wasn't so much that the penny dropped but a whole safe was thrown off a cliff: the bus had left and we were alone. You've never experienced true loneliness until you're crouched in a cold Missouri ditch.

'Help!' I shouted (finally) into the dark. Well, half

shouted. A polite shout. 'I've been kidnapped. Seriously. Anyone?'

There was no reply but the sound of the wind through unseen trees. I'd not panic. And I'd not cry either. Positive mental visualisation. A comfortable seat in a coach to LA. But the warming image made me feel even more anxious. Sometimes I hated myself.

'Come on,' said Jennifer. 'Follow me somewhere with heating at least.'

I touched the tip of my nose. It felt like an ice cube.

The road we walked was too large for the amount of passing traffic. Every so often we'd hear the approaching roar of an engine behind us or see the growing intensity of headlights up ahead, appearing like twin meteorites rushing in parallel to the ground. And we'd hide, sliding down an icy, damp verge to disappear. And, every time, Jennifer was more interested in the safety of her package than me.

Shivering in my T-shirt, checked shirt and jeans, I became more and more definite in my decision.

The first chance I got, I'd tell a responsible adult what had happened. I was half tempted to flag down a car, but I was as likely to get hit as noticed. It was one of those long roads in the middle of nowhere that (I thought) only existed in movies. If there was a speed limit, the motorists weren't interested in keeping to it.

It hadn't snowed around here or, if it had, the snow had melted. The air remained piercing, though, and the idea of not only my coat but all my possessions speeding to California without me was in no way warming.

As I walked, I thought back to the airport, of how close I'd been to catching the connecting flight. How warm, how happy, would I now be if Nicolas Cage hadn't intervened? There's a sharp lesson to cut yourself on.

What started as a pinprick on the horizon grew in time to a pool of light. This shone brighter the closer we got. Eventually the light split and focused into three neon signs: GAS! MOTEL! TEXAS BBQ!

'Are you still cold?' asked Jennifer.

I was shivering too much to answer properly, so just grunted.

All three places were wild with illumination, a supernova in the night sky, like they were competing to use up the most electricity. The Texas BBQ bled light and music into the night and Jennifer launched directly for it.

My stomach rumbled in excited anticipation. Little

did it know. In the parking lot, which is American for 'car park', Jennifer paused next to a pick-up truck.

'Wait here. Move and you're dead,' she said. (She had a way of making threats seem genuine. It was her eyes. So intense.) 'And don't lose the box. I'm trusting you.'

And she was off. As she pulled open the restaurant door, the night rocked with music and laughter for the few seconds before the metal and glass swept shut behind her. I thought about resting the box at my feet but didn't want to risk an argument. Maybe it would blow up if not warmed by human contact? Who knew?

My hands stung with growing numbness. How cold would it have to be to get frostbite? Was my nose still there? I'd seen horrific pictures of failed mountain climbers. I tried moving my nostrils but could feel nothing. Losing my wallet was one thing but I'd hate to live out the rest of my life without a nose. People would point and give me nicknames. Noseless J. Face. Skellboy. Voldemort.

Maybe this was my chance. I looked to the gas station. I could see an attendant through the glass. A phone lit her face. At some point Mum would try ringing me. What would she do when she couldn't get through? Would she worry? Would she contact the British Embassy? Dad would tell her to get a grip. Dad would understand that I'd messed up.

The BBQ door smashed open and out exploded Jennifer, running. She threw a thick, black coat at me. It covered my head and smelt of man.

'Come on!' she said, pulling at my elbow. 'And don't drop that parcel.'

She was wearing a red trench coat. It opened out like a cape behind her. I followed its sweep to the motel. We ran past the neon arrow pointing at reception and continued into a courtyard, in the middle of which was a swimming pool.

Steam rose lazily from still water. In the corner of the space was a bracket with a hose wrapped in its centre. Jennifer pulled us behind this and we slammed to the floor, our backs to the brick of the motel wall, hiding and out of breath.

The chemicals from the pool spiked the air. An engine sounded from the gas station on the other side of the motel. I hugged the stolen coat like a toddler with a security blanket. We were hidden. Unless anyone in the motel rooms opposite decided to look out of their windows.

Our breathing blew hot clouds like speech bubbles. When we'd caught our breath and there was no obvious shouting or footsteps from angry, coatless restaurant customers, I stood up and cleared my throat.

'I'm really sorry,' I said. 'But I'm cold and I'm tired. And stealing isn't cool. I should be on the Greyhound. I won a competition.'

'*Cool*,' she said. 'What are you? Thirty-nine? Who says cool?'

(She was laughing.)

'Lit, then. Lit AF. Whatever you're meant to say and, anyway, I'm going to the motel reception now. It was nice meeting you.'

'You don't have any money, do you?'

'Not to book a room. To hand myself in. To just, you know, let them know what's happened. I'll say you ran off into the night. Don't worry. I'm not a snake.'

'What *has* happened?' she asked.

'Honestly? I don't know. It's like I've fallen into an alternate reality.'

She smiled, the bare opposite of the words that followed.

'You broke my wrist, Jay. That happened. Not comic books.'

'It's Jacob. And I don't want to argue but you weren't looking where you were going. That's not my fault. I'm sorry. And, anyway, I think we're probably even by now. I dropped my voice. 'There's no way it's broken.' I stood, batting away her (good) hand from its grasping. 'I don't want to get into trouble. You talk about your grandmother but you've not met my parents. They'd both die if they knew what was happening.' She continued to smile. 'Why doesn't anyone take me seriously over here?'

'Who's your favourite superhero?'

Of all the things she could have said, I never expected this.

'What? Why?'

'Just answer, Mr Salty. Thirty seconds delay in ratting me out won't make a difference.'

I sat back down.

'Spider-Man. And I'm not ratting you out.'

'Peter Parker's his real name, right?'

'Right.'

'I always preferred Peter Parker to Spider-Man. Less pleased with himself.' And she sucked her bottom lip before saying, 'Anyway, do you think either Spider-Man or Peter Parker or whoever would give up on a stranger who'd asked for help? A stranger who promised they weren't doing anything wrong. A stranger whose wrist they'd broken?'

My mind shut down, broken by the obvious emotional blackmail. When I was able to talk again, it was in a somewhat/slightly pleading tone.

'You're wanted by the police, Jennifer. And being chased by some psychopath cowboy man. And –' I looked down to the box, imagining it brimful of golden necklaces and platinum rings – 'who knows what you're hiding in there.'

'I'm not telling you, Jay.'

'Why not?'

'It's personal.'

'Will you at least say why you're going to LA?'

'Sure. To see my dad. He's at Twin Towers Correctional Facility, four hundred and fifty Bauchet Street, Los Angeles. So are you going to come with me or what?'

I'm not going to lie; what she said had some effect. And, maybe if I'd been in the middle of the Somerset countryside, and not somewhere between Missouri and California, I might have helped her out.

Standing, I put the coat on. It hung from me like a cloak.

'I'm sorry,' I said. 'I need to be in that movie. And,

as soon as I've spoken to someone who can help me out of all this, I'm going to return the coat to the restaurant. Somehow. It's just really cold, so—'

And I took two steps from the flashlights of her eyes before a man, wearing a baseball cap and no coat, palmed his hand against my chest.

'Hella sick coat, bro. Where'd you get it?'

CHAPTER 12

Angry Coatless Man

Of all the people Jennifer had to steal from she chose this guy. He stood with a chest like a prison wall. Under his left eye there was a tattoo of a skull and the skull was crying. He was more like a video-game character than a real person.

I'd like to say I squared up to him. But if I had done, I'd have only reached nipple height. Instead I stammered and sidestepped. And, as I stammered and sidestepped, he mirrored my movement. There was no passing him – to the left was the swimming pool, to the right the motel.

'Sorry,' I said, my mind empty of suggestions for what else to say.

Jennifer got to her feet, struggling to lift the package.

Her face shook with shocks of pain. Without thinking I reached out to help, taking the box from her unsteady grip.

'So let me tell you what I'm going to do. I'm gonna take these coats off you. And then I'm going to beat loverboy here so hard he's gonna be swallowing eyelashes for weeks.'

'Bite me,' said Jennifer.

'How about we just give you the coats back and you forget about it?' I asked, smiling so he knew I wasn't the bad guy. 'There's been a misunderstanding.'

'You bet your Aussie ass there's been a misunderstanding. You been misunderstanding whose coats you stole.'

Jennifer stepped towards him. I don't know what she was planning to do, but whatever it was she didn't get very far. He raised a hand and gently bounced her back.

'Easy now,' he said.

With the same hand still outstretched he beckoned me forward.

'So how about you show me what's in that box?' he said.

You won't believe it, because I can't either, but I said 'no', adding, 'It's not yours.'

'Them coats ain't yours neither, buddy.'

He lunged for the box. As he did so, I turned my left shoulder. I didn't step into his chest. It was more that he bounced off me. I must have really rubbery muscles or something.

But contact was made. Contact that forced him to stumble backwards. His feet got tangled – we've all been there. One second he was standing, the next he was swinging his arms to find balance. And if he hadn't been back-stepping towards a swimming pool, he might have been successful.

His body hit the water with a rip through the night, his cap spinning off like a stolen Frisbee. Before I could process what had happened, Jennifer slapped my back.

'Run!' she called, flying past.

We left the courtyard, passed the reception and emerged into the parking lot. There was a coach, about three-quarters the size of the Greyhound, at the gas station. Even in the dull light of the forecourt, it was clear the vehicle had seen a few scrapes. Its facing side was undulated with bumps. A group staggered around it as someone stood at the rear filling up. I thought maybe it was a drunken party going home or even a group of old people with mobility issues, but as we jogged closer we saw what they were.

Zombies.

Jennifer's pace slackened only slightly.

Clothes were ripped and skin was peeling. The zombie at the pump turned her head to the other zombies, calling instructions.

'Don't hold your arms so straight! Put your tongue away! Try dragging your feet!'

We ran towards the undead and Jennifer jumped up and through the coach's door. As we were being chased by a mad, wet, angry man I didn't think there was anything else to do but follow.

Inside, there was darkness but no passengers.

They must be all outside, practising their moves, I thought.

'Hide in a footwell,' said Jennifer. 'Nobody ever sits up front. Quickly.'

I dived into the black space between two banks of chairs. My hands moved over crisp packets and disturbed a sharp stink of foot sweat. Jennifer disappeared in the corresponding space on the other side of the aisle.

'Hey!' A voice shook the outside world and echoed against the coach windows. Instantly the groaning stopped. 'You seen two kids? Wearing big-ass coats?'

'Sir, are you okay?' came the response, a woman's voice. 'Do you need assistance?'

We should have dumped the coats.

'We should have dumped the coats,' I hissed across the aisle, but the darkness said nothing back.

The man roared his question again. 'I said: have you seen two kids?'

'I saw a pair heading towards the store,' came a response from outside, another voice. 'Running. I don't know. Maybe you need to calm down.'

There was a moment of silence before a muffled banging came from the rear of the coach.

'Guess that's practice over,' said the original woman and soon after the coach trembled with bodies getting on board.

I didn't breathe. I closed my eyes as tightly as the lids allowed. I rested my head on the package, praying there was nothing explosive inside. Wrapping my arms round my chest, I found comfort in the soft padding of the coat.

The zombie passengers got back on and when the coach's door hissed closed, I knew I should say something. Because I was a stowaway on transportation for monsters.

A pair of legs stood in the aisle, centimetres from my nose. They ended in a pair of Converse, dull in the night. Had I been caught? Or worse: was their owner about to sit on me?

'We all okay? We set? Any more bathroom breaks?' said the legs, a female voice.

'This costume's a nightmare to get off in the restroom,' came a reply from the other end of the bus.

'You should have worn diapers,' said someone else. 'Mia did.'

Laughter rippled across the seats. Laughter that came mostly from the rear of the coach.

'I've lost a nose,' said someone else. 'Anyone seen my nose?'

I checked my nose. It was present. That was something, I thought, as I looked past the legs. Jennifer's space was so dark it was like she wasn't even there.

As the coach laughed and someone asked if there were any Doritos going spare, I hissed across the aisle. 'Jennifer!'

There was no response. The legs spoke again.

'I know it's awful late but how about we try a go at "Tomorrow", just to lift our hearts as we pull away? I know our driver would love it.' There came some rumbling from the driver's seat, a noise that didn't sound full of enthusiasm. 'You all know your parts, you total babes.'

The Converse walked off. The coach growled to a

start. As it did, the passengers broke out singing. And the toothy sort that splits your skull because it's so annoying, with the singers smiling like there's a gun pointed at their family and they've been ordered to look like they're having fun.

'Just thinking about tomorrow clears away the cobwebs and the sorrow,' they sang.

Okay, so we'd escaped a violent beating, but being trapped on a bus full of musical-theatre-loving zombies wasn't, like, a huge improvement.

I dared stretch up, lifting my head so that my eyes were level with the bottom of the window. The seats hid me from being seen. Across the forecourt, I saw a figure in silhouette, the bright neon behind him.

It was the Cowboy, standing there, watching us.

PART 2

WEDNESDAY

TIME UNTIL THE MOVIE SHOOT:
27 HOURS 7 MINUTES

Jazz Hands
Oklahoma

'Yo, you can get up now.'

How I fell asleep, down in the crumby, cramped space between two seats, I have no idea. But fall asleep I did. And now that Jennifer was waking me, I felt that instant panic of not knowing where I was, of expecting to see my bedroom wall, the Spider-Man posters. Instead there was this American girl I hardly knew, who was, like, seventeen and standing in the aisle with the Converse-wearing zombie woman.

It all felt a bit overwhelming to be honest.

Jennifer's arms reached out, but not to help me. She wanted the box, which I'd been using as the world's least comfortable pillow. I lifted my head from it. The right side of my face was tooth-out numb. My brain pounded.

'I've explained everything to Nicky,' said Jennifer. 'About running away from Tulsa. But how our parents didn't even notice so we're giving up and going back. Nicky's been real chill about it all. And . . . umm . . . she really likes musical theatre. Like really.'

'Good morning, good morning!' sang the woman.

Pulling myself from the space, I noticed three coins shining where I'd slept. I picked them up and offered them to her.

'Keep it, honey,' said Nicky, looking at me with a strained smile.

I pulled myself into a seat.

'Thanks,' I said. 'I've got a killer headache.'

'I hope you're not going to suggest it's our singing.' She did some fake laughing, then continued. 'So I don't know if you noticed,' she said in an unreasonably loud voice that sounded like an exaggerated impression of an American accent, 'but we're all dressed as zombies.' I nodded. I *had* noticed. 'We're down from the Missouri State musical theatre programme and we're heading for Tulsa. And it's *so* much fun already. Rooooooooooad triiiiiiiiiiiip!'

Nicky did a little clap and jiggled her shoulders. The pain behind my skull increased by 33 per cent. She had a strange face. Her muscles were pulled tight and almost shivered with the energy required to hold the smile. Her eyes didn't look happy, though. There was, like, a spark of panic behind them. She wore two huge earrings that were each a block of text. Both said I STUDY MUSICAL THEATRE. WHAT'S YOUR SUPERPOWER?

'Road trip!' she said again and pretended to play a saxophone, I think. I looked to Jennifer. She shrugged. 'There's a zombie walk happening. Do you know what a zombie walk is?' I shook my head, even though I had a fair idea through understanding the words 'zombie' and 'walk'. 'People dress as zombies and they walk around. It is so, so neat. Like, oh my actual God. Can you even imagine?'

'Sounds like the bomb, right?' asked Jennifer.

'Yes,' I said. 'It does.'

'Today in Tulsa they're trying out for the world-record largest zombie walk. I mean, we wouldn't miss it for the world. Well, unless it clashed with a *Hamilton* tour! The only way I could imagine it being better is if the zombies could sing but I contacted the organisers and they were worried about disturbing local residents, which I can totally understand. Still, go, Missouri! We are *so* blessed.'

Nicky put her hands together in prayer, closed her eyes, and muttered silent words.

Jennifer stared. A serious face. 'Nicky's said we can stay on until Tulsa, Jay.'

The singer's eyes snapped open. She raised a finger. Its nail had very bright red varnish.

'*Uno* conditiono. I can't have *dos* young runaways on my conscience, even if I am dressed as the undead! Hahahahaha. Someone ought to record me.' She looked down the aisle. 'Who's got a voice recorder?' A few people held up their phones. She flapped a hand. 'I'm kidding, I'm kidding. I am *such* a kidder.'

Unbelievably Jennifer's face got even more serious.

'Nicky's going to dump us with the first police officer she sees.'

It was my chance to flash my eyes in disbelief as Nicky said how she'd said nothing about dumping, how there'd be no dumping, no siree.

'Safely handing over to state officials to ensure your safe return home,' smiled Nicky. 'I believe that's what I said.'

'I thought we were going back to our home in Tulsa,' I said. 'To our parents?'

'Whoa there. What's with the accent?' asked Nicky. 'Are you an actor? Do we have an actor on board? Selfieeeee!'

'My brother's back from boarding school in England. Our parents are Harry Potter mad.' Nicky narrowed her eyes. 'Also, he's adopted.' Jennifer drew a circle round her face. 'You might have noticed the slight colour difference.'

'One: I'm colour blind, actually,' said Nicky, staring. Eventually she broke from her trance and wagged a finger. 'And two: I'm cursed with this tremendous, fantastic conscience. It's a blessing as much as a curse and it wouldn't let me sleep if it knew you weren't being looked after. Three: don't think I've forgotten about that wrist. You need a professional to take a look-see, young lady, if it hurts as much as you say. Now, has there ever been a musical set in a hospital? What a killer idea!' She began singing again, as she wandered up the aisle and away from us, doing jazz hands. 'Thigh bone connected to the hip bone! What's that tune? It's a banger. Hip bone connected to the something bone.'

'Maybe it would have been better to have been beaten up by angry bro at the gas station,' said Jennifer.

'Less painful,' I said.

Later, sitting alone up front, we hissed conspiratorially, our conversation obscured by the singing, which had inevitably started up again. Every so often, the driver would side-eye us from his rear-view mirror like he knew the truth.

'We've got a lift to Tulsa,' said Jennifer.

'What about LA?'

'Tulsa's on the way.'

'Really?'

'Why you always got to question me about everything? We'd be, like, beating the Greyhound if these musical losers hadn't picked up friends in Kansas City.'

'What do you mean?'

'You know all the stop-offs and dinner breaks built into the Greyhound schedule? They add hours. If we just keep on heading west, we'll be there this time tomorrow, I swear.'

'What time *is* it?'

Jennifer looked into the grey gloom past the bus's windows, something like a murky fish tank.

'Dunno. Early.'

Silence fell between us. Partly because of the unreal situation. A bus full of musical-theatre-loving zombies on the way to Tulsa. When I spoke, it was to avoid thinking about it all.

'Marvel did a zombie series once.'

'There's a zombie everything these days,' said Jennifer.

Nicky appeared, killing stone dead what might have been a good chat. She wore an expression like there was an invisible hornet on her nose. There were dark crescents under her eyes but they kind of added to the zombie feel to give her credit.

'You two want to get involved? Dumb question! Of course you do! Like, obviously.'

'Involved?' asked Jennifer like she'd never heard the word before.

'In the singing, girlfriend! You picked the wrong bus to play stowaway on if you don't like singing.'

Jennifer stared her out. 'Well,' she said eventually, 'I *don't* like singing. Especially before breakfast. But my brother here's a choirboy.'

'I'm not singing,' I said. 'No way.'

'Okay,' said Nicky. 'How about I hold my breath until you agree?'

She filled her lungs. She nodded. She pointed at her face as it went from pink to red to purple.

Jennifer kicked me.

'Okay,' I said.

Nicky's mouth burst open for air, a fish out of water.

'Seriously?' she said, after she'd caught her breath. 'I was close to dying there. You Aussies!'

'I'm not Australian.'

The bus rumbled on and, two minutes later, I was standing in the aisle, holding a microphone given to me by the driver. I also held the head of an empty seat to stop me toppling as the unrelenting wheels bounced over potholes.

And, yes, it was cringe and, yes, it was embarrassing, but I reasoned I should be past caring by now. And I *had* been in a choir at primary school and my old head teacher *had* said I showed a lot of promise. Nicky swore the bus would join in as soon as they recognised the tune, so it wasn't as if I'd be singing alone.

I cleared my throat. Speakers crackled. Jennifer did a comedy wink.

I sang the first line of the theme song of the 1960s *Spider-Man* TV show.

My voice sounded tiny and shaky. Maybe there was a problem with the microphone? Like it was on the 'baby' setting?

'Ummmm, okay,' said Nicky really loudly.

Jennifer covered her face with her hands. Her shoulders jumped with embarrassed laughter. But I'd show her. She'd not be laughing when the bus joined in.

I persevered, I was resilient, a quality they're always banging on about at school.

The zombies gawked. Most mouths dropped open, but none with singing as Nicky had promised.

My voice tremored even more violently as I began the third line.

Nicky stood from her seat and grabbed the microphone.

'Let's hear it for . . .' She frowned, dropping the microphone from her mouth. 'What's your name again, hon?' she asked.

'Jacob,' I replied, my cheeks exploding in pink shame.

'Jacob! He gave it a good go, didn't he? A good go, Jacob.'

'Thanks.'

The zombie passengers clapped for a bit. I returned to Jennifer. Her eyes were watering.

'I am *so* sorry,' she said and pulled me in for a hug.

(Which almost made the embarrassment worthwhile. Almost.)

'Who knows *The Greatest Showman*?' yelled Nicky into the microphone.

The bus went crazy.

Lipstick
Catoosa, Oklahoma

We passed a blue whale. Beached at a lake, its mouth was open to the shore. The thing was about 75 per cent realistic because whales can't smile and even if they could, there was nothing about this one's situation to make it happy: alone, far away from the ocean, misunderstood. Also, it looked like it was made from painted wood.

Maybe, once upon a time, it'd been travelling to Hollywood.

We were on Route 66, which used to be world-famous, according to Nicky. The coach slowed as the passengers raised their phones to the window. Jennifer wasn't interested. She was too busy putting on make-up. Specifically zombie make-up. She'd borrowed a mirror and when she was done, she turned and asked what I thought. I gave a thumbs up. She looked terrible.

'Your turn now,' she said, thrusting a stick of lipstick at my face.

I edged further away, my back flush to the window.

'I know what you're thinking. Should she be wielding heavy lipstick with that wrist? Well, Jay, maybe I have made a big deal about it. But, you know what, maybe . . . I was worried that if you weren't feeling guilty, you'd not stick around.'

I hadn't expected that. I felt a weird warmth inside my chest. She lunged with the lipstick.

'I don't want to,' I said, but smiling.

'You must,' she replied, smiling too. 'Normal is not an option. We're going to hide in plain sight. As zombies. That's the plan.'

'I thought the plan was getting to LA?'

'Tulsa's closer to LA than Chicago. Trust me.'

And then Nicky appeared at Jennifer's shoulder, killing the smiles. She was good at appearing exactly when you didn't want her.

'Everything okay?' she said. 'You two hungry? I bet you are. I was thinking. There's only brains on offer when we get to Catoosa. Ha! I'm joking, of course. I can get *so* kooky sometimes. You don't have to eat brains. Here.'

She handed over two apples and a couple of packets of crisps.

Jennifer thanked her. 'Just doing Jacob's make-up,' she said. 'We don't want to be arriving at the zombie walk not looking right.'

'Brains,' I said, and Jennifer rolled her eyes.

Nicky looked like she wanted to say something – I knew how she felt – but, instead, she wandered away. I let Jennifer have a go with the make-up. I was learning that it was easier to agree than put up a fight.

(Her face was really close to mine.)

The site of the zombie walk was a high-school sports ground. As the bus rolled into the complex, it was quickly obvious that PE in America was different from home. There was an actual stadium here with banked seats and everything. I think I'd end up a school refuser if they took sports this seriously in Somerset. As would the PE teachers.

Jennifer didn't seem bothered. Maybe because she was American; she'd seen it all before. She wasn't even that fussed about the ranks of emergency vehicles lining the entry road.

It was an avenue of four squad cars, two each side, four ambulances, two each side again, and two bright fire engines facing each other. Had the authorities brought their oldest operational vehicles to tie in with the zombie theme? Each one looked fifty years out of date and were so battered they seemed sad.

'Loads of police, then,' I said.

She nodded. 'But if I were the type to worry, I'd worry about the Cowboy.'

'Really?'

I hadn't told her about what I thought I'd seen at the gas station. She'd launch a hundred questions I couldn't answer. The coach swung into a lot lightly sprinkled with other vehicles. Its brakes hissed.

'Where are the zombie hordes?' asked Jennifer, frowning. 'I thought this was meant to be a world record or something.'

'We're kinda early,' said Nicky, swinging out of a seat and taking a sudden microphone from the driver's outstretched hand. 'Well, good morning, everyone. Rise and shine! As you can see, we're here and we're premature. But that's fine cos there should be coffee somewhere, but I'd like us to all travel in one group if possible. You know the rules! Teamwork makes the dream work! LOL. So make sure you've your name stickers on and don't go leaving any valuables behind. Because I'm a kleptomaniac! Joking, joking. But really – don't leave any valuables. I've got to say farewell to our two runaways here and then I'll see you outside shortly. Thanks, you guys.' She made like she was handing the microphone back to the driver, then swept it back to her mouth. The speakers whined in protest as she screamed. 'But before we go . . . one last "Time Warp", people!'

'Hold this,' hissed Jennifer as she shoved the box into my chest. 'Don't talk, don't sing, follow me. Closely.'

As Nicky conducted the choir with swinging arms, Jennifer stepped behind her and I followed. The group leader had her eyes closed in appreciation of the song's beauty. We tiptoed past the driver, who was sitting with his head in his hands, his elbows balanced against the steering wheel. (I felt like if we were nice, we'd take him with us.)

The bus sang as if the lyrics were straight out of the Bible or something.

There was a huge red button on the dashboard. Underneath it was the word 'exit'. Jennifer, no idiot, pushed it. Jumping from the bus, we headed away from the police and their cars. We rushed towards an American football pitch with the devil-horn goals and maybe half a dozen zombies meandering around. We travelled faster than any members of the undead had ever moved and continued to speed as we passed through a group of confused-looking (and decomposing) students.

'Almost there,' said Jennifer, checking over her shoulder that there were no jazz hands grasping for us.

Over the other side of the grass, in a corner between two stands, was a flat one-storey building. Outside this was, although not a crowd exactly, a gang of zombies. As we got closer, their Styrofoam cups, gripped tightly, came into focus.

We pushed through double doors, tumbling into a movie vision of a high-school canteen. It was the kind of place where jocks throw rotten apples at spotty geeks. Today, however, the plastic benches supported a threat of a different kind: zombies. And loads of them.

'I think we made it,' said Jennifer, out of breath in no way. She gestured at the space and the zombies. 'Check this out.'

I managed to get two words out between two deep breaths.

'Well . . . dench.'

Jennifer frowned. I'd not use that word again.

'Say what?'

'"Dench" means good.'

Her frown deepened like a rockfall.

'Y'know, I'm beginning to understand why we fought a war to get rid of you guys.'

There was a zombie scrum at the far end of the hall fighting for free coffee and doughnuts rather than dead bodies.

'Injured child coming through,' called Jennifer and although it was a risky tactic what with us being suspected criminals on the run, the crowd parted. Jennifer was soon back with a paper plate of doughnuts.

We took a nearby bench, sitting shoulder to shoulder between two groups, with an uninterrupted view across the canteen and the doors leading outside.

And we'd not even had time to take a single mouthful of the frosted doughnuts, and, man, did they look good, before the doors swung open and in stepped the Cowboy.

CHAPTER 15

Brains

Jennifer dropped her doughnut. With sugary fingers she grabbed my arm.

'No,' she hissed, eyes widening. 'Come on! We've just got here!'

The Cowboy was alone. He wore that same denim jacket. And – there – the hat. If anyone else had been wearing it, they'd have looked dumb. But not him. It transmitted a threatening authority. Already the hall's conversation had dropped, simply because of the heavy vibes radiating from the man and his brim. Did he have a gun? Was there a gun under that jacket?

'How'd he even know we were here? Maybe he's got, like, spidey-sense.'

(I immediately regretted saying this.)

'Okay, so this was always going to happen,' said Jennifer, regaining control over herself. 'Just act normal. Eat a doughnut. We're zombies. He won't recognise us. Maybe it's a coincidence. Maybe he's into horror movies.'

(Her left leg bounced with nervous energy.)

Without people on the opposite side of the table there was no hiding. It was like we were framed by the space, the emptiness inviting his attention to fall on us. I willed myself tiny. I'd apologise if he caught us.

'What I did, sir, whatever that was, was wrong. And I'm really sorry.'

Sometimes, if you're really apologetic, people don't get that angry.

With narrow eyes the Cowboy inspected the hall. But . . . all he could see was the undead. He stepped a tentative snakeskin boot on to a bench and climbed up on to the table. A pair of zombies, drinking coffee, stared in disbelief. Doughnuts were suspended in mid-air, nobody dared chew. I tried not to stare at him but it was difficult to pull your eyes away.

'Attention, zombies!' he called. 'Please! For one second!' He didn't need to repeat his request. 'Jennifer Lewis, are you there? Answer me, sweetheart.'

His voice rumbled like thunder. Zombies looked to each other. The table groaned under the Cowboy's feet as he shifted his weight. Jennifer and I, we bowed our heads and pretended to be fascinated by our doughnuts, sitting frozen. (But my heart was beating loud enough for her to hear, I'm sure.)

'Just came in on a coach from Missouri. A boy and a girl. Runaways. Have you seen them? I've a wallet full of cash for anyone who has. You see, my employer is a very generous woman.' He paused. The room murmured. 'Call out if you're here, kids. Or raise a hand. Surrender now and you'll save yourself a great deal of trouble. Jacob? Jennifer? Help an old man.'

His eyes flashed across the space as someone brave called out, 'Are you the police, sir?'

'No,' said the Cowboy and I'm sure he looked straight at us. 'I'm the gentleman you sure don't want to be running from. Thank you kindly for your time.'

He climbed down from the table. His footsteps echoed like gunshots as he strode to the exit. We watched him push back through the doors. When they swung closed behind him, it didn't feel like victory. I'll tell you what it did feel like: like defeat had been paused for Fate to put the kettle on.

'Right,' I said to Jennifer, swallowing my anxiety/ doughnut. 'So, that was close.'

'Were you scared?'

'I don't know about scared. Just, you know, not whatever the opposite of scared is. Brave? Is brave the opposite of scared? I'm rambling,' I said. 'I do that.'

'I've noticed. It makes you sound scared.'

'I'm *so* not.'

'You're *so* British it's unreal.'

The corpse make-up on her cheekbones only made her eyes shine the more intensely. I looked to the sugar that frosted the table. I didn't want to argue.

'I can't believe I sang on the bus,' I said quietly as I stared at the sugar, feeling again like all we were doing was running from an avalanche of trouble, a trouble avalanche. And the thing about avalanches is that they always catch you. Unless you're in a helicopter or on a motorbike or . . .

'The singing was savage.' She shone a full-beam smile my way. 'Jay, are you not enjoying this? We were sitting *right* in front of the Cowboy and he didn't see us. We got away. The plan worked. So we'll finish breakfast and we'll sneak out the back and grab a bus or taxi or whatever to Tulsa. Don't sweat it.' She could see I was unsure.

And I could see that her leg was still bouncing. 'This is your origin story. You're like—'

Words burst from me like water from a fire hose.

'I'm no superhero. Please. And if I were, I'd be, like, Worry-Man. Because all this is going to end with me in massive trouble. I can feel it. I'm *not* enjoying myself. And if your wrist honestly hurts, you should go and see a doctor. Like the musical theatre person said. It's not good. None of this is good. It's bad. I'm a kid. It's not the same for you. Maybe I am *so* British and that's why you don't understand.' Pause. 'Because you're not.' Jennifer looked confused. 'British.'

'I've kidnapped you, remember. You won't get in trouble.' The zombie closest to us looked over. Jennifer lowered her voice. 'This is all new for me too. Straight up. When's your movie happening? That's the important thing, right?'

'Tomorrow afternoon.'

It sounded impossibly close, California impossibly distant. For the first time missing it felt more likely than not.

Jennifer nodded out a response. 'I can get us there by then. No problem. It'll be as if nothing happened. Just a little detour. And as soon as we're in LA, we split. My wrist *does* hurt but it's just . . . it's just . . . it's more of an adventure when there's two of us. A real adventure too. Like . . . Bonnie and Clyde. Or Batman and Robin.'

'What about the Cowboy?'

'He's not caught us yet, has he?'

I stood from the table, brushing sugar from my top. I left her box next to the coffee.

'I'm going to the toilet,' I said. 'And I don't even know who Bonnie and Clyde are, by the way.'

(Obviously I did – they're characters on that Cartoon Central show.)

'Bathroom,' she said. 'Toilet sounds gross.'

Two thumbs up. Toothy smile. Even though I shook my head, I couldn't stop a 25 per cent grin. I kind of hated Jennifer for it.

Maybe I'd ask her again what was in the box when I got back. Maybe she'd tell me now. Maybe I was enjoying myself.

(When I returned, she had vanished.)

CHAPTER 16

No Tears

The table was full of strangers wearing basketball tops streaked with (fake) blood. *And* there was no box. And definitely no Jennifer.

Great.

I steamed up and down the aisles, like I'd lost a parent in the supermarket. But there was no box on any table. There was no Jennifer anywhere. I returned to where we'd been sitting. Maybe she'd gone to the toilet too? I waited awkwardly. Eventually a basketball guy turned round. Blood oozed from his mouth. His eyes were a milky white.

'You okay, bro?' he asked.

'You've not seen a girl, have you, please?'

The group's attention focused on me as the guy grinned. My skin tightened.

'You're a Brit? A Brit zombie?' I nodded. 'Good for you. And I've seen plenty girls today. You need to narrow it down. *Cherchez la femme*, right? Ain't that the truth.'

'Yeah.' (Whatever that meant.) I described Jennifer. 'And she was holding a box wrapped in brown paper.'

He shook his head. He asked his friends. Nobody could help.

She'd probably decided that it was best to split up. I wasn't a great travelling companion. My main skill was being able to hold stuff and a bag can do that. She didn't even laugh at my jokes. I mean, I'd dump me if I were travelling with me. I make me miss planes and I make me make stupid decisions.

Alone, I stepped out into the morning. Each breath further inflated the question WHAT NOW?

Across the football field, zombies warmed up. The air, less cold than Chicago, was rippled with soft moans of 'braaaains'. And, then, at the other side of the grass, I spotted something terrible.

It wasn't a person being ripped apart by hungry monsters. Worse: it was Jennifer being marched by two police officers towards the battered emergency vehicles. Even from this distance, I could see she was struggling, her braids whipping across her back as she moved. Inevitably the Cowboy walked alongside, a good foot taller than the others. He left a trail of cigarette smoke behind him – the white puffs punctuating his path like steam-train smoke.

The cops took Jennifer to an all-black squad car. As they reached it, the group turned. The Cowboy held the box. The rear door of the car was opened. One officer put his hand on Jennifer's head and lowered her in like they do on TV. He slammed the door and the noise shuddered across the space, echoing against the empty stands like a firecracker. The two police officers shook hands with the Cowboy and soon their car edged away from its space and disappeared off through the far gate and on to the supposedly famous Route 66 and a different story.

And, standing there, I felt like I was being gradually lowered into a tank full of cold water. The wetness was anxiety and it rose over my ankles, over my waist, over my head. I screwed my hands into balls. I bit into my bottom lip. I forgot how to breathe.

'Where am I? And how did I get here?' I wanted to shout.

But I didn't. Because strangers would turn and strangers would look at me. And that would make things worse. The looking.

The Cowboy got into a black pick-up, his mission

complete. Frozen, I watched it roll away and, as I did, I shivered. She'd been caught. My partner in crime. Bonnie. What now? What next? What happened to Clyde? Did he have a happy ending?

First off, I wouldn't cry. That would be a terrible mistake, no matter how much my throat tightened and my eyes stung. (Loads.)

At least she'll get her wrist seen to.

But she'd looked . . . desperate. I mean, I hadn't seen her face but her shoulders were slumped. And the thing about Jennifer is how full of energy she always was. The sugar sparkle. Like she'd shotgunned a dozen energy drinks. No slumping.

And now she was gone. And I was left alone. How was I ever going to free her from a police car? I was a kid, a thin-limbed loser, who'd once got himself locked in a school toilet for three periods (it was only French and everyone thought I'd done it on purpose) but . . .

Here's the takeaway: I was no hero. I was a massive idiot.

The only sensible option was to call home. Mum and Dad would tell me what to do. It didn't matter that ringing them didn't *feel* right.

Probably. Because where had feelings ever got me?

Phone Home

I asked a zombie with a clipboard if I could borrow her phone. I'd guessed she was an organiser and not a random wearing a dead-office-worker costume. She also had the thin lips of someone who enjoyed data entry.

'Why?'

For once in America I tried honesty. Well, partial, at least. I smiled an asking-the-teacher-if-I-could-go-to-the-toilet-mid-lesson smile.

'I need to call home.'

Her forehead wrinkled. 'Are you Irish?' she asked.

I couldn't deny my heritage. Dad would go crazy. (And it was a change from Australian.)

'English,' I said, hoping this was a good thing.

'Have you ever been to Brighton? I've got friends in Brighton. The Haydens.'

'Brighton is nice,' I said. She looked like she wanted me to continue. 'But I've never been.' She continued to look like she wanted me to continue. 'And I've never met anyone called Hayden.'

Her face crumpled in disappointment. I kind of wished I'd lied.

'Well, there's probably a payphone in reception. Sorry I can't be of more assistance.' She pointed across the field. 'Right now, I've a coach load of Boy Scouts missing in the Osage reservation. You'd think they'd be good at map reading.'

I hurried in the direction she indicated, trying to not think about where Jennifer might be heading, the interrogation rooms with single naked light bulbs. Instead I practised what I'd say to whoever picked up the phone back home.

'Don't be angry because I've not done anything wrong. I'm still on my way to Hollywood but I don't have my phone or my wallet. Could you ring the studio, please? I'm worried I'm going to miss my scene. Like, if I'm really unlucky. And it's totally not my fault. Maybe they could send a car or something? I was helping out a friend. Thanks, then.'

I pulled at the reception door. It was locked. I felt a bit teary again and tried to ignore the images of Jennifer's face that kept appearing in my thoughts like a weird, broken Netflix stream played in my mind.

Don't cry, don't cry.

'What you after, junior?'

A man in blue trousers, a blue jacket and a blue baseball cap stood with his hands on his hips. Each item of clothing held the school's crest.

'A payphone,' I said.

'You Australian?' he asked. 'I didn't know you could get Australian zombies.' I couldn't be bothered to correct him, so I shrugged. 'Reception's locked down today on account of security. The school doesn't want the undead wandering around its insides, you know what I mean? Who does? And, anyway, the phone's not worked since 2012. Vandals. The closest payphone is down McNabb Field Road,' he said. 'Straight out of here. There's a Hampton Inn. Won't take you five minutes.'

I said, 'Thanks.' He said, 'You're welcome.' Neither of us meant it.

Despite its name, the Hampton Inn wasn't a pub. It was a hotel and my breathing relaxed when I realised this. There'd be no drunken Americans shouting at me. Or fewer, at least. From the outside the building looked fairly new, the ground floor clad in interlinked slabs of stone, like caveman Lego, and the rest of the tall structure was a stark white. It sat off the main road like a shipwrecked ferry.

Shoulders slumped, I walked in, hoping my undead appearance wouldn't upset anybody. Because, I told myself, this was the correct decision. I. Was. Doing. The. Right. Thing. Clapping emoji.

The man at reception didn't blink. He turned from his desk computer and said that his name was Henry and he was looking forward to helping me. He had a voice like a mosquito whine.

'Thanks,' I said. 'My name is Jacob. And I'm looking for a payphone.'

'Absolutely no problem at all,' he said. 'If you care to turn round, you'll see there's one behind you, sir.'

He wasn't wrong. It was attached to the wall in a darkened corner. A thin plastic shield arched over its boxlike body.

I lifted the handset and fed my musical-theatre-bus coins into the grey plastic. Taking a deep breath, I dialled home, not forgetting the international code. Had I ever used a payphone before? I'm not sure I'd even *seen* one outside of TV.

Mum answered. Her voice was as clear as if she'd been standing next to me.

'Hello?' she said.

'Mum, it's Jacob!'

'Jay! Where are you?'

She didn't sound *that* excited. I was expecting more excitement. Rehearsed lines ran through my mind.

'Great. Oklahoma, I think. Anyway . . .' There sounded a distant beeping sound. 'I've lost my phone.'

'You're not in Hollywood? What's the problem? Are you okay?'

'The bus.'

Mum sighed. The beeping grew in volume. The LCD screen on the payphone said 'add more credit'.

'What about the bus?'

'It wasn't as fast as the plane. And America is so big.'

'Jacob? Is everything okay? Don't panic me.'

'I'm safe. It's like an adventure.'

'Mothers don't like adventures. Why aren't you in Hollywood already? Is it still snowing? Are you going to arrive in time? Imagine if you . . . your dad . . . are you eating, Jacob? Are you keeping hydrated?'

'Everything's okay,' I said. 'I've lost my phone, that's all.'

'Jacob? What's the meaning of this?'

It was Dad. And I'd been full ready to admit everything, to explain how scared I felt, how alone, in the middle of the middle of America, surrounded by musical-theatre-loving zombies and strangers who thought I was Australian. I was on the edge of confession. Of asking what I should do. But I couldn't shake the feeling, a pulling sense somewhere near my heart, that I'd let Jennifer down. That it was my fault she'd been caught.

And, honestly, I think her wrist *really* was troubling her.

'Hi,' a new me said. 'Just ringing to say hi. That's all.'

And the beeping stopped. And the phone's screen flashed CALL TERMINATED. I'd run out of cash.

'Right,' I said. 'What now?'

But there was no answer in the phone's droning tone. I'd have to decide for myself.

CHAPTER 18

Bacon

Replacing the handset, I stared at the numbered buttons.

Life is easy when it's simple. Wake up. Go to school. Come home. Go to bed. Routine. Somerset, my laptop, WhatsApp messages, the Marvel Insta account, Charlie in the year above with the smile and the tan.

In Geography once we read about these teenagers in the Amazon, who get given, like, these drugs made from herbs and plants and are then cast out into the jungle. They go crazy for forty-eight hours, hallucinating and all sorts, and return to the tribe as adults.

Was that what was happening to me? If the adults I know are anything to go by, adult life is rubbish. They don't get grey hair as a natural part of ageing. Colour is drained from them by the stresses and strains of being old.

Still, feeling sorry for myself, feeling guilty about Jennifer, neither was going to get me to California. I went to Paris with school once and we'd been told to go to the British Embassy if we were in trouble. I didn't think Oklahoma had a British Embassy, but I might have been wrong.

A voice broke through my muddled thinking.

'Howdy, partner. How are we doing for rooms? I need somewhere to freshen up.'

The Cowboy. I couldn't believe it. What a day. I wanted to roll up into a ball on the floor, maybe even suck my thumb. Did a tiny bit of wee escape? Possibly.

'My name's Henry,' said Henry the receptionist, 'and I'm here to help. To answer your question, we've plenty, thank you very much.'

I tried to shrink into the shadows. Even though I hadn't been his target, I didn't want to get lassoed back into trouble or whatever it was that cowboys did.

'One with a bath would be grand,' said the Cowboy.

Henry told him that all rooms came with an en-suite shower. The Cowboy said that sometimes these days he didn't recognise his own country. Next they fussed with cash as the Cowboy swore that plastic cards were the devil's own invention.

'There's no breakfast going spare, is there?' he asked, having been given his room's keycard.

(Was it still only morning? Time goes slowly when you're on the run from the law.)

'Well, we're still serving, sir. Ten dollars gets you the European buffet.'

'What's that?'

'Croissant and orange juice.'

'Your man not able to fix me up some bacon? I've been on the road all night.'

Henry said he'd see what he could do and pointed the Cowboy in the direction of the restaurant.

'Are you wanting to check in any luggage, sir?'

'This here box is worth more than your whole hotel, no word of a lie,' said the Cowboy. 'So it's staying with me. And it's all the luggage I've got. Learnt how to travel light, you see. No change of pants even. Denim's not intended to be washed. You know that, Henry?'

The box! He'd obviously been sent after that, not Jennifer. The police were dealing with her now. And the lump in my throat told me that this way round wasn't necessarily better.

What *was* in it? Would she have ever told me? Drugs or money, those were the two most likely options. Now

I'd never find out. This was turning into the worst trip ever.

I waited for the Cowboy to leave. As the footsteps of his boots faded, I slipped from the shadows and escaped the building.

I had no idea where I was going. I just knew the Cowboy scared me and I needed a non-scary place to come up with a plan. Down the road was a shopping park. Buildings huddled around a lot spotted with cars. I was kind of thinking I'd see if there was anything helpful around, some abandoned plane tickets maybe, before giving up.

In a daze I wandered into a place called GNC. There were shelves full of vitamin pills and nutritional supplements. Maybe there'd be something that could turn me super strong and super fast. I'd be able to rescue Jennifer. A man, in GNC-branded uniform, came over.

'Hi,' he said.

'Y'all right?' I replied.

'I'm awesome, thanks for asking.' (Now wasn't the time to tell him I wasn't *actually* asking, but it was how you say 'hi' in the UK.) 'Do you need any help?'

'Just browsing,' I said.

'For what?'

'Super-strength pills?'

Sighing, the man pointed at the door and said maybe it was best I leave.

Outside, there was a new vehicle across the tarmac: another black police car. I noticed it straight off. Was it placed there for me? I'd not broken the law. Was running away from cops criminal? Wearing a stolen coat? I *had* lied about my age to get on the Greyhound, but they couldn't throw me into jail for that.

Could they?

The cops might not believe my story but they'd have to do something about it/me. Because they were the law. And also adults. *And* I had an English accent and was wearing zombie make-up.

I would surrender myself unconditionally to the mercy of law enforcement.

Because the only alternative I could think of was settling down in Catoosa, trying to get a job to pay for food and, in time, maybe getting married and starting my own family.

And, on balance, I'd rather risk being shouted at. I mean, there might still be enough time to get to Hollywood. *And* there was English homework for next week that I hadn't done.

The car was parked outside a restaurant called Taco Bueno. Decision: the best thing to do would be to wait for the officers to come back from getting a breakfast burrito or whatever. But as I approached, as slowly as I could walk without actually stopping, I realised that I'd seen its bumps before and, not only that, but there was definitely somebody in the back seat and, not only that, but . . . it was Jennifer.

The bright red collar of her (stolen) coat shone like molten lava.

No way.

My legs froze as my heart leapt. What now? And where were the police? Could I get her out? *Should* I get her out? I'd not felt this confused since the last Physics progress test.

And she turned. And she saw me. And she lasered those bright eyes directly into my face and her high eyebrows could mean only one thing.

GET ME OUT, FFS.

She waved through the rear windscreen. She wasn't wearing handcuffs. Probably because she'd moaned about her wrist. I took a few slow steps forward, conscious that the police could emerge from the Mexican restaurant, like, at any second.

Already I was at the side of the car. Jennifer's face was up against the window, fogging it with hot breath. Her mouth opened like she was screaming but I could only faintly hear what she said.

'Get me out, you dumbass Brit!'

I shrugged. I didn't have the keys – what was I meant to do? She raised a hand and pointed down, at the outside handle, with a violent finger. Her eyes flared as I tried it. The door opened. She pretty much tumbled out.

'My hero,' she said, not, if I'm honest, sounding much like she meant it. But she definitely meant what came next – a big hug. She fully threw her arms round my awkward frame and grabbed me tight. 'Thanks, bruh.'

Jennifer was warm, really warm. And soft. Before I could process what was happening, suffocating, as I was, in an avalanche of muddled feelings, she let go.

I wanted to speak but all that happened was stammering. And, anyway, Jennifer was telling me, once again, to run. Somewhere in between getting caught by the police and being released by me, her arm had been put in a makeshift sling, made from a black-and-white bandana. I had no time to ask her about it, though, because she was already off.

As she headed away, I looked back to the restaurant. There was no sign of the law. Why hadn't they locked the car? Why hadn't Jennifer opened the door? Were there child locks? Couldn't you open the rear doors from the inside?

America was v. confusing.

Already she was on the other side of the lot. I closed the car door gently. As it clicked shut, the rear bumper dropped with a sharp crack against the tarmac.

'Hey!'

A police officer, with a coffee in one hand and holding a brown paper bag in the other, stood in the Mexican restaurant's doorway. He had a shaved head and a huge hipster beard and didn't look happy to see me trashing his car.

In that instant, he reminded me of Mr Roberts, my Year Eight Biology teacher. Everyone was terrified of Mr Roberts. And in his lessons we'd learnt about the fight-or-flight response. It's a psychological reaction to a perceived threat. Our bodies flood with adrenalin as we decide whether to make a stand or to run away.

'Yo!' shouted the man. 'Freeze!'

I turned and sprinted after Jennifer.

'Sorry!' I shouted over my shoulder. 'But I've been kidnapped!'

And, to be honest, despite everything, I was smiling.

CHAPTER 19

Wet Pasta

As I lay in a wheelie bin, abandoned spaghetti soaked through my coat. The stink of cheese sauce was overwhelming, especially as this coffin's* lid meant the smell had nowhere else to go.

(* Not an actual coffin.)

It'd be bad to die this way, overcome by the toxic fumes of melted Cheddar. My death might become a meme. It'd be all over Twitter like a rash.

'Stop fidgeting,' hissed Jennifer. 'They'll see.'

I wasn't fidgeting. I was as still as a corpse, even though we'd been in here for at least ten minutes. I counted to two hundred in my head. It took my mind off the smell and meant there was a verified pause before I spoke next.

'Let's get out,' I whispered. 'I'm going to vom.'

Given the choice, I think I'd prefer to die than throw up over Jennifer. Imagine how embarrassing that'd be.

'What's wrong with you?' she said. 'Are you, like, six or something?'

As she spoke, late-morning light flooded the bin. Someone had opened us up.

A thin teenager, wearing the red-and-white stripes of the Italian restaurant that owned the hiding place, stood holding a black bin bag of doom above us. He let out a high-pitched scream.

'What?' said Jennifer. 'Some privacy maybe?'

He shook his head. He said sorry. He let the lid drop.

'I guess that means it's time to leave,' groaned Jennifer from the gloom.

We pushed the lid up and rolled out. As we straightened ourselves, spaghetti plopped to the ground in a shower of dead worms. The teenager stood gawking.

'You've not seen any police, have you?' I asked. 'Or a cowboy?'

He shook his head, probably trying to process my accent.

'They had a vehicle here five minutes ago but it left with its siren blasting. I've got to return to the kitchen, guys.' He tapped his nose. 'I won't tell the manager about you, though.'

He deposited his bag in the bin and disappeared through a fire exit. Jennifer pulled off her (stolen) coat and flapped it free of pasta. I took my coat off and copied Jennifer. With each shake the smell of cheese grew stronger.

After we put the coats back on, she looked at me and I looked at her and she pointed at my face.

'You've penne on your forehead,' she said. 'Penne head.'

I flicked it off, smudging the white zombie make-up underneath. If Jennifer's face was anything to go by, I must have looked a nightmare. Half Halloween, half dinner.

'So why *were* you in the police car?' I said, definitely not admitting that ten minutes ago I was about to hand myself in, sounding like I was making conversation and was, like, totally chill about everything.

'Why do you think? The Cowboy gave me a choice. Either I go back to Illinois with him or I go with the cops. I chose the cops. I figured it gave me a better chance of escaping. And it looks like I was right. Hot dog!'

'Where?'

I ran my fingers through my hair.

'No. You know.' She slapped a thigh. 'Like, *hot dog*!'

Occasionally I wondered whether Jennifer was crazy. Or maybe acted that way down to all this being a huge prank with me as the victim and hidden cameras everywhere?

'You might be free,' I said, 'but you'll never escape . . . a criminal record?'

(I remember a visiting police constable using that in assembly once.)

'Yeah, Grandmother won't ever let *that* happen. Anyway, you're a criminal too now. Destroying police property like that. I saw a new side to you. The real Jacob. Scary.'

'The bumper fell off,' I said. 'It just fell off. I didn't do anything. It. Fell. Off.'

Jennifer laughed. She had a particular sense of humour: anything that made me look bad was funny. I decided to tell her something that'd stop her laughing.

'Anyway, I saw the Cowboy. He had your box and was saying how it was worth more than the hotel.'

Instantly: 'What hotel?'

'The one up the road.'

'And he had the box?'

'He did.'

And, once again, she was off. And as I watched her braided ponytail sweep like a metronome across the red shoulders of her stolen coat, I wished I'd said nothing. Don't tell anyone, though: I was pleased she was back.

I caught up with her as she headed directly for the hotel, like a shark rocketing towards a surfer's leg.

She stopped, eyes flashing. 'Are we a team, Peter Parker?'

'Don't call me that,' I said. 'It's cringe.'

'What's "cringe"?'

'You know, like cringe-worthy? Like awkward. Like that feeling under your skin.'

'I'll tell you what's cringe: are you with me or not?'

'Yes,' I said.

'Yes what?'

'I'm with you.'

'You *know* I'll get you to Los Angeles, right? We've all got appointments to keep. And you're going to be a movie star, remember.'

I didn't see how chasing after the Cowboy was going to help but, stranded here in Oklahoma, I had little alternative.

Before we entered the hotel, I was expecting Jennifer to brief me. Gang leaders do it in films with chalkboards. I guess modern gangsters use *PowerPoint*. Something, anyway. Some plan of attack.

Nothing.

'Hi, I'm Henry, and—'

Jennifer spoke over the receptionist. His smile vanished in the blink of an eye. I stood behind her, having never felt so far away from home, wanting to turn invisible so badly right now.

'We're looking for a cowboy. He has something that belongs to us.'

(*Us.*)

Henry narrowed his eyes. 'It's company policy not to—'

Jennifer broke in again. This time, her voice had all its edges rounded off.

'He's my grandfather,' she said, 'and he gets confused. Thinks he's a cowboy. It's so very sad.'

Henry stared. I looked down to my feet as the air around us grew awks. There was spaghetti on my left toe. I scraped it off with my other foot. I had a sudden panic that we'd left a trail of pasta that the police could use to track us. But a glance over my shoulder showed the entrance to be spaghetti-free.

'Okay, so he's in the restaurant, finishing his breakfast,' said Henry. 'He insisted on bacon. Is he always so . . . Western? It *is* sad. No offence.'

'None taken. Because it is *so* sad.'

'I'm soooo sorry,' said Henry, his eyes dropping to his screen and his fingers tapping at an unseen keyboard. 'That can't be fun.' He paused. 'So sad.'

Jennifer thanked him and pulled me away.

'You distract the Cowboy,' she hissed. 'I'll grab the box.'

A sign on the wall pointed in the direction of the restaurant.

'Distract him how?'

'Dress up as Buffalo Bill? I don't know. You'll think of something. You're creative. With the poem and the . . .'

The Cowboy sat with his back to the wall, spooning yellow into his mouth and holding a folded newspaper. He wore half-moon glasses at the end of his nose. They made him look more like a grandparent than a US marshal (retired).

On his table, next to half a glass of orange juice and a bottle of ketchup, was the box, as innocent as your mum's Amazon delivery.

Jennifer spun us to the opposite wall, shutting off the Cowboy's side of the restaurant from sight.

'Ready?' she hissed.

I looked to the wall ahead. It was as blank as my mind.

'I . . .'

Smiling, she pushed me forward.

Hard Croissant

As soon as I crossed into the restaurant, I fell to my hands and knees. Hidden from the Cowboy, I shuffled towards the buffet table. The carpet scratched under my palms like it was trying to persuade me that the plan was stupid.

But what the carpet didn't know was that I didn't have a plan. Not yet, anyway.

Doctor Manhattan can stop time. That'd be sweet. I could break for a muffin. I'd love a muffin. A blueberry one.

Past the legs of tables and chairs I could see the Cowboy's boots.

I crawled under the buffet, then popped my head out from beneath the grey tablecloth, the fabric resting on my hair like a headscarf. The Cowboy was immediately to my right, past four empty tables.

I dared to glance towards the corridor. There was no sign of Jennifer.

On the buffet table was a plate of cold pastries. I'd seen them when crawling. I reached up and grabbed something flaky with icing. It was satisfyingly hard, like it had been sitting on the table for days. Without so much as a deep breath I launched it like I'd chuck a video-game grenade: up and over.

It missed the Cowboy by a good two metres, landing unseen with the faintness of a fairy's fart.

I took a croissant. I squeezed it to manufacture a more streamlined missile. Again I lobbed it. The spirit of a dead basketball player must have temporarily possessed me. Dad would have been proud. The croissant hit the Cowboy's newspaper with a satisfying rustle.

I ducked down, grabbing more food as I did, my heart bouncing like a toddler on Haribo. As there wasn't an immediate reaction, I dared peek out from the tablecloth again.

The Cowboy was slowly folding the paper, unhurried and unfazed. He took his glasses off, closing their arms and placing them delicately on the table. As he looked in my direction, I ducked away.

'It's too early for funny business,' he growled. 'Who's there?'

I could taste adrenalin and, weirdly, it tasted of Coke. I threw the next pastry. My eyes focused on the Cowboy's snakeskin boots. I've no idea where this shot landed, but it had the desired effect. The boots kicked out as his chair squeaked from his table.

'I see you, partner. What's your game? If there's one thing I don't like, it's wasted pastries.'

A crunch of furniture came from the other side of the room. Through table legs, I glimpsed the quick blur of Jennifer. I stood up. The Cowboy faced me, looking for all the world like he was about to draw a six-shooter. I grabbed a further fistful of croissants and threw hard.

The golden flakes didn't stretch half the distance and, from beneath his walrus moustache, there came a smile. 'I had a feeling we'd meet again.'

'Hello,' I replied and I didn't say sorry, even though his ten-gallon stare was making me feel massively apologetic.

Instead I kept my focus on the Cowboy. I didn't want to betray Jennifer's presence by looking away. He'd stepped from the table. Here was her chance.

'It's lucky for you I'm in a good mood, son. Time was there'd be hell to pay if someone threw a croissant at me.' I still didn't apologise. 'You don't know what you're caught up in.' The Cowboy moved back to his chair. He placed a thick hand on the box. Jennifer should have grabbed it when she'd had the opportunity. Now things were complicated. 'Big stakes, son. And I'm not even sure your new best friend knew what she was taking in the first place.'

'It's not yours,' I managed.

'Sure, it ain't. But it's not hers neither. The rightful owner, a woman of influence, Jennifer's grandmother, paid me to do a job. I promised to get it done and as a man of my word that's exactly what I'm intending to do. Straight after I finish this paper and get me a few hours of shut-eye, see.'

'But—' I tried.

'We can't all be the hero. And the girl's already miles distant. In police custody too. You twig?'

He sat down. I heard Jennifer sigh. The Cowboy heard too, his head snapping in the sound's direction.

I needed to distract him.

'She only wants to see her dad.'

His attention returned its spotlight to me.

'Is that what she told you? Hell. This is America. Every one's got a hustle. I was sent to retrieve the package, not the girl. You might want to think on that.'

There was a doughnut, the last item on the plate of breakfast pastries. It was pregnant with jam. And it was my final shot.

I grabbed it.

'Throwing a doughnut isn't going to get your friend back,' he said. 'But it'll surely rile me.'

I pulled my arm up and behind my head, just like a pitcher.

The Cowboy smoothed his moustache with the fingers of his left hand.

'Let's not get any funny ideas,' he said with a gunpowder rumble.

Too late! The cake had already left my hand. It soared, a sugary meteorite. And he was up and out of his chair as . . . the doughnut passed harmlessly over his shoulder, hitting the wall with a red squelch like someone had been shot in the head.

It was now that Jennifer moved. She sprang like a jack-in-the-box and swept the package from the table one-handed. The Cowboy clutched at thin air, knocking over his juice as he did, the glass clinking as it hit the table.

'Come on!' called Jennifer, already halfway across the room.

Disaster! My left foot caught a table leg and I went flying. From the floor I saw two things. One: Jennifer hesitating, eyes flashing with panic. Two: behind me, the Cowboy looming. He stretched out his hands.

My legs kicked in a desperate pedal to get me up and away. Tread caught carpet and I launched forward, the Cowboy's fingertips sweeping across my (stolen) coat but failing to grip.

I banged into another chair and sent it cartwheeling into the Cowboy's path.

'Goddamnit, kids!' he roared as we disappeared into the corridor.

'Hey, is there a bus stop nearby?' Jennifer called to Henry as we flew through reception, the box now passed to me.

'Out front,' said Henry as we fell through the automatic doors into the sharp Oklahoma day. We left him calling, 'Where's your . . . ?' at the exit.

Half a football pitch away, a bus rolled to a stop. We pumped muscles to catch it. We were within touching distance, our chests bursting with hot breathing, when its engine farted into action and it started to pull away.

But . . .

miraculously . . .

after six metres . . .

it stopped.

The door opened. We clambered on. Jennifer suddenly had a fistful of change and she fed it, one-handed, into the ticket machine's mouth. The bus driver, a round woman with a smile larger than her face, looked on.

'You two leaving the zombie thing already? You're lucky I saw you.'

'The place is dead,' replied Jennifer without even a hint of a smile.

Adults say travel changes you. That's why rich kids have gap years. And if you'd told me four weeks earlier that I'd be on the run across America with a mysterious girl who may or may not be transporting drugs or money or whatever, I'd have had a panic attack at the very idea.

But heading towards Tulsa, I looked out of the window at fields spotted with lonely trees and I enjoyed the familiar Weetabix glow that came with being back on the road with Jennifer.

We swapped buses on to a Greyhound in Tulsa. Jennifer had shown me what she'd found in her stolen coat pocket: a wallet full of credit cards and ID for a Miss Gonzalez. And whoever this Miss Gonzalez was, she had a carefree attitude to security. There was also a scrap of paper with a list of PINs.

'When were you going to tell me about this?' I'd asked.

'I'm telling you now. I thought you knew, anyway.'

She used one of the cards to buy Greyhound tickets. I wasn't even nervous because I was so sure the attempt would fail. For one thing, the woman on the driving licence had a different-coloured face to Jennifer (even without the zombie make-up). And, seeing how it'd been some time since the wallet had gone missing, surely the woman would have cancelled her cards?

Apparently not. And neither did being done up like the undead affect our chances of purchasing tickets. That's American customer service for you.

After washing off our zombie faces in the restrooms, we picked up supplies. Water, crisps, chocolate, the kind of stuff your parents would never let you buy. Using the stolen credit card was bad, okay. But, first off, Jennifer was the one who'd done it and, secondly, she swore that when we got to California, she'd tell her dad to pay back the cash.

'So, technically we're not stealing, we're borrowing.'

I don't know about you, but I was hundo P convinced by the argument.

CHAPTER 21

The Box
Route 66, somewhere in the Texas panhandle

We were back on the road and Jennifer said, 'So do you want to know what's in the box?'

'Yes!' I replied instantly and urgently. Enthusiasm is not a good look. I added, 'I guess. You know, if you're cool with it.'

'My mom's ashes. There. I said it.'

I yelped. I can't think of any other word to describe the noise. Judging by her expression, Jennifer wasn't a big fan of the yelp.

'What did you think it was?' she asked.

'I don't know. Drugs?'

Cue laser beams from her eyes burning straight through my face. Guilt crept over my body like an army of stick insects. Her mum's ashes. Not money. Not diamonds.

Five minutes later, on the floor, at our feet, was the brown cardboard box – slightly more battered than it had been in Chicago. And on my lap, a wooden urn.

Out of its packaging, it felt heavier. I tried to keep completely still. I could see Jennifer trembling.

'Wow,' I said. 'Okay.'

Question: how would you react if you had the ashes of someone's mum on your lap? In an urn, okay, but still. Growing up, we're told in school assemblies, is all about learning how to deal with new and confusing emotions. If that's true, I'd done my fair share of maturing on this trip.

Now I felt a combination of gross out and, like, massive sympathy for Jennifer, whose mum wasn't only dead but also ashes, which is pretty final.

'I'm so sorry,' I said. 'I won't open it.'

'No, you fricking won't. And I wouldn't let just anyone hold it, by the way, so . . .'

To be honest, I wanted to hand it back and quickly. I'm not a robot, though (at least, I don't *think* I am), and doing this might have upset Jennifer. Instead I looked at the thing and nodded and said, 'It certainly puts things into perspective,' because I remembered Mum saying that when next door's dog died after eating six chocolate Easter eggs.

Jennifer nodded. Jennifer agreed. It did.

'How did she . . . ?'

As soon as I spoke, I regretted it. It was so sad, like too sad to comprehend. How could anyone ever cope? Your mum. I should have said something to cheer her up. I hadn't mentioned the Nicolas Cage picture in Chicago airport. Was that funny? I knew loads of jokes . . . like the one about the zoo with only a dog in it.

'She was cremated, Jacob. It's like five thousand degrees or something.'

'No, I mean . . .'

She reached out to place a hand on the urn. I sat as still as I'd ever sat. It would be disrespectful to fidget.

'I *know* what you mean.' She looked directly at me. 'She was going to the store. She . . . she just stepped off the kerb. And a car hit her. The guy wasn't speeding. He hadn't been drinking or anything. Mom just stepped out. She hadn't seen him.' She pulled back her hand. 'She was going to the store. To get milk. And then she died.'

Language abandoned me. What could I say?

'That's bad,' I said. 'Like, really bad.'

Jennifer frowned. 'It *is*, Jacob.' Her voice strained with anger. 'Dad was away. He's in the army. Was in the army.

Because Grandmother—' Suddenly she softened. 'You don't need to know all this. I don't know. Why don't we talk about *your* family?'

'What's her problem? Your grandmother? Lex Luthor?'

I wanted to sound interested and caring. Because I *was* interested and caring.

'She doesn't like me. I mean, she thought the best thing to do with a kid who'd lost her mom was to send her to boarding school. In her world, money is what solves things. Even hurt.'

'I'm sorry, Jennifer,' I said, imagining dormitories.

'Not as sorry as me. Anyway, it's not your fault.'

Obviously she was right. But that didn't stop me feeling bad. And it also didn't stop two questions flaring in my mind:

1. How did Jennifer's dad end up in prison?
2. Why was her gran so keen to recover the urn of ashes, even sending a US marshal (retired) after them? *And* he'd said the package was worth more than the hotel *and* I don't think he was talking, like, spiritually. I mean, we're getting away from an actual question now, but you understand my point.

'That's enough real talk for today. You've seen it. It's my mom. She's dead. She belongs with Dad. And that's where I'm taking her. He got out of the army last month. It's time.' Jennifer turned to the view of rolling nothingness through the glass past me and said, 'I've spent years promising myself I'd do this. And here I am. But I never imagined a bus full of musical zombies. I never imagined getting into a fight over a stolen coat. And I never imagined you, my English sidekick.'

Was she crying? Were her eyes watering? Maybe it was the air conditioning? Everywhere is air-conditioned in the States. She was definitely chewing her bottom lip again. I lifted a hand from the urn and put it on her shoulder. It was a strange angle and felt awkward. Jennifer didn't respond. I patted her once, twice. On the third pat she turned.

'What are you doing? I'm not a dog.'

I stopped the patting. But it was okay. 'I'm going to help you,' I said.

We put the urn back into the box. I tried not to think about home, about how I'd feel if my mum died. It wouldn't be great, to be honest. I got out the potato chips and offered the packet.

Jennifer shook her head. 'Is that all you think about?'

'What?'

'Food?'

'No.'

Because it wasn't. Because we'd not even had a proper breakfast. Because sometimes I think about other things too.

CHAPTER 22

Wellington, Somerset

'If we stay on the bus, it'll take thirty-two hours to get to Los Angeles.' Jennifer picked at her nails, which took some doing in a sling. Hers, like mine, had specks of black under their white crowns. 'Meaning . . .'

She brought a finger from her good hand up to her mouth and bit a nail. As she did this, I did the maths. The numbers demanded some proper thinking, so I even used my fingers *but* made like I was inspecting my nails, inspired by Jennifer.

Calculation conclusion: we'd get to LA late Thursday afternoon. Which would be bad, seeing how my scene was due to be shot at midday.

'So I won't get to LA in time? I won't get there by twelve?'

'Not if we stay on this bus.'

Anxiety bubbled through my blood. I tried to stop thinking. I imagined my mind a blank canvas, a ceiling, a page of my homework diary. Because the last thing I wanted to be doing was imagining telling Mum and Dad that I'd missed the shoot. That would be worse than imagining missing the shoot.

Why hadn't I stayed in the Chicago hotel? Like everyone else. The normals, with their normal decisions. Why'd I ever decide that getting on a Greyhound was a good idea?

I felt my heart begin to shift and wriggle against my ribcage. Sweat broke from my forehead. I needed to shift focus. I needed to calm down. I needed to start a random conversation.

'You live in Chicago, then?'

'Yeah. Kinda. You live in London?'

'No. A place called Wellington. It's near another place called Taunton. It's the other side of England. Which is like the distance between two neighbouring towns out here, I guess.'

'Right. What's it like?'

'It's, *like*, really crap.'

'No kidding?'

I dropped my voice like I was announcing the most shocking piece of gossip ever.

'It doesn't even have a McDonald's.'

She *was* shocked.

'No way.'

'It sucks. But there's a drive-through in Taunton, so . . .'

'I'd kill for a peanut butter and jelly sandwich right now. Like, literally kill.'

The look in her eyes meant I completely believed her. Maybe food was all *she* thought about.

'A what?' I dared.

'A sandwich is two pieces of bread—'

'No,' I interrupted, 'the other bit.'

'You've not heard of peanut butter? Is England medieval?'

'I mean, yes. I've heard of peanut butter. But I've never tried it. It sounds gross.' I had a vision of melted butter with broken nuts inside and, to be honest, it didn't look very appetising. 'It's the jelly bit. Doesn't it fall out? Or just, like, wobble?'

'Okay, so tell me what you think jelly is.'

'Red. Wobbly. You have it with ice cream on your sixth birthday.'

'Right. That's Jell-O. Jelly's a spread.'

'Like jam?'

'If you say so.'

My half-reflection stared back from the window, an untidy ghost. It was thinking about Hollywood, about missed opportunities, about stupid decisions. But mainly about strawberry jam on toast.

'So, anyway, Jell-O aside, we'll get you to LA on time, no problem,' said Jennifer. 'Because there's something I've not told you.'

Was she pranking me? Was this a prank? You never knew. Whatever, I had to control the puppy excitement bouncing in my chest.

Chill and Zen, Jacob.

'What haven't you told me?'

'We're not taking the bus all the way. I was thinking we could get a plane.' Full-beam Jennifer stare.

I pretty much choked on my crisps.

'Say what?' I asked. 'How much will *that* cost? Are you pranking me? Is this a prank? You're pranking me, right?'

(I mean, planes *are* quicker than buses.)

She raised her eyebrows, meaning, of course, that we had a credit card and so money didn't matter. And, no, she wasn't pranking me.

'It'd take, like, two hours to fly to LA, Jay. Two hours. You get to Hollywood by today, I get to Dad before I'm caught. All this could be over by tomorrow. And the neat trick is they won't be looking for us in airports. They'll assume we're on a Greyhound. Because we are. Think about it. We're on a bus for a day – that's a whole day we're likely to be caught *and* you miss your scene. If we're on a plane, we have two hours to worry through and, boom, we're in Cali tonight.'

I didn't say yes. But I didn't say no either. Because, like diamonds, Jennifer's eyes sparkled and, also like diamonds, they were so hard it meant there was no point arguing.

Also – a plane *would* mean arriving on time, which was all kinds of okays.

'And the Cowboy hates planes. Anyway,' she added like it was nothing, 'our bus tickets are only good for travel to Albuquerque. Where the airport is. And part of being a superhero is taking risks, Jay. It's not just Superman who flies. People do it all the time over here. It's probably like trains in the UK. Or horse and carriage. No biggie.'

I wiped my hands free of Lay's Sour Cream and Onion and thought about how best to respond.

'A: Wolverine's scared of flying. B: I don't like trains.'
I paused, then: 'C: Will they let me on the plane? I'm
fourteen.'

She was looking out of the window as she replied, her
reflection grinning.

'Course they will; you, me and Mom too. It's like a
family.'

We had hours to kill. And loads of them. Jennifer slept
through most. I found a book in the seat pocket. It was
a child's version of a story called *The Odyssey* by a long-
dead man called Homer, who I'd heard of because of
The Simpsons. Someone had probably bought it for their
kid, thinking it perfect reading for a long journey.

I dipped in and out. The hero had it easy – he was
only trying to get home. It would have been a different
story if he'd been on his way to Hollywood.

Delta Force
Albuquerque, New Mexico

We were in New Mexico, a name for Google images of strange rock formations and cacti shaped like quick-draw cowboys, but it remained (stolen) coat-wearing weather. As it was night (again), the only cacti we saw were neon ones on the walls of supermarkets lining the dark drive to the airport.

Jennifer marched us to a Delta desk. At the Tulsa Greyhound station I'd been sure that the stolen card would be turned down and that FBI agents would step from the shadows. (Didn't happen.) As we waited for the rep to deal with a man whose tuba had been damaged en route from Atlanta, I asked Jennifer if she'd still admit to kidnapping me, should we get caught.

'We're not getting caught,' she said.

'But if we do?'

'We're not.'

'But—'

She held me squarely with one of her fly-killing looks.

'How old are you?' she asked.

The question made me feel about five.

'You know that. I'm *almost* fifteen.'

She stared like she was scanning my thoughts. And then the man with the tuba moved on and we stepped up. The Delta rep's smile hadn't diminished an iota.

'Jennifer?' I said.

'Okay, okay. I've kidnapped you. Jeez.' The Delta dude *so* heard but Jennifer didn't care. She addressed him, single raised eyebrow, with the sort of confidence that could freeze blood. 'We'd like two tickets to Los Angeles, please. On the next available flight.'

'And I'd *like* your ID. Please.'

Jennifer handed over the stolen driving licence. They waited, watching, as I scrambled to get my passport out of my inside pocket. Sometimes I hate my fingers.

'Miss . . .' The rep paused to find the name on the ID. 'Gonzalez?' Jennifer nodded. 'What's your relationship to . . .' He opened my passport. 'Jacob here?'

'Family friends.'

The Delta rep nodded. But it was the type of nod that meant anything but acceptance. He indicated the sling.

'How did you injure yourself?'

'Falling over a princess.'

The Delta rep didn't miss a beat.

'Too bad. And it says here you're twenty years old?'

'Uh-huh.'

'And you're accompanying this child?'

(I mean, it took a while before I realised he meant me and surely there were a hundred other ways to ask the question? Like, in a way that didn't make me feel as if I should currently be watching toy-unwrapping videos on a Kindle Fire, for instance.)

'Yep.'

The Delta rep looked from the driving licence to Jennifer. I could feel my everything shrink – partly through anxiety and partly through awkwardness. Next there came keyboard tapping and the airline man, instead of telling Jennifer that all this was crazy and we were about to get in truckloads of trouble, announced that the next flight to LA was in ninety minutes.

'How will you be paying today?'

Jennifer handed over the stolen card without speaking. Delta slipped it into a payment machine and Jennifer entered the PIN and no alarms sounded and no FBI agents appeared. The total cost of our two flights was less than the bus ticket I'd bought in Chicago all those millions of years ago.

Boarding cards were printed and, nope, we had no luggage to check, just the carry-on plastic bag, and we were told our gate number and that was that. We stepped away and Jennifer pulled her (good) arm through mine. Smiling like I'd never seen her smile before, she said, 'Did you see how the Delta dude asked about my hand? He felt sorry for me.'

'Your dad will *definitely* pay for it all?' I asked.

'Yes!' said Jennifer. 'I swear James Bond's never like this. What about the queen? She's chill, right? Quit worrying. We've done it. Best decision ever. The key is keeping the act up.'

We decided to eat before braving the security checks and, kind of inevitably, we ended up at McDonald's. Jennifer had her nuggets with BBQ sauce, and I had a quarter pounder. It tasted great. Proper American but not too much. The table next to us was a group of sad-eyes who half-heartedly juggled nuggets. They wore sweatshirts with NANTUCKET CLOWN SCHOOL 2020 printed on them. Normally this'd be massively distracting.

'Sorry,' I said, even though I wasn't. Pause. 'About being negative back there.' (Awkward gear change.) 'So . . . you ever been to LA before?'

'No. I've heard a ton about it, though.'

'Well,' I said, 'we can enjoy the sights together. There are the stars in the pavement, right? And the sign on the hill – Hollywood. All that stuff. I bet there are some good burgers too. Umm . . .'

As cringy as I sounded, my words did the trick. Jennifer smiled. There was even a kiddy bounce to the way she walked down the airport corridor.

'They have In-N-Out. And I'd like to see Venice Beach. Huge dudes lift weights there. Imagine. Wonder how hot it is. It'll be sunny, I swear.'

I mean, I wasn't overwhelmed by the thought of huge dudes but I didn't want to kill the vibe, so: 'Yeah,' I said.

We'd been getting on well. She'd told me about her mum. I'd made her smile. A couple of times. I watched her wipe her hands on a serviette. There was a sauce spot in the corner of her mouth.

'Why's the Cowboy so desperate to get the urn?' I asked.

Jennifer screwed the serviette into a ball. She sucked

from the straw of her soda (which is what Americans call fizzy drinks – I was literally learning a new thing every five minutes). When she was done, she locked in her stare and said, 'Because it contains my mother's ashes, Jacob. We've been through this.'

I picked at an abandoned fry like what I was about to say didn't really mean anything. So casual.

'But the Cowboy, back there, he said it was worth more than the hotel and I don't think he meant metaphorically.'

'You still don't understand, do you? My grandmother . . . she's a proud woman. Scary too. Terrifying. And, you know, my mom was her daughter, so . . .'

She must be scary, I thought, *to have a US marshal, retired, doing what she orders, not to mention the police forces of at least three separate states.*

Jennifer reached past abandoned pickles and empty sauce sachets to touch my hand. At girl contact blood rushed to my cheeks and I hoped she thought it was because of a mustard allergy or something. I could feel the chip grease on her fingertips and I didn't even care.

'Look,' she said. 'We're actually doing this. So, for the last time: quit worrying. It's not good for your mental health.' She withdrew her hand. I murmured something into my chest. 'When I first met you, I can't even say how lame I thought you looked. I mean, I hadn't realised you were English back then, but still . . .'

'Thanks,' I said.

'I'm trying to be complimentary. It's not something that comes natural. You've ketchup all over your mouth, by the way.'

'Tomato ketchup gets everywhere.'

'*Tomato* ketchup? What other type is there?'

I rang home from another payphone, one that accepted cards. I told Jennifer that it was safer to check in than have my parents worrying. There was no knowing what they might do, who they might call.

There was a chemical smell to the air as I waited for someone to answer.

'Yes?'

It was Amy. My spirit dipped.

'Is Mum there?'

'No. She's asleep. It's, like, six in the morning, Jacob.'

I'd forgotten about the time difference.

'How come you're awake?'

'I've just got back from a crazy night out. You wouldn't understand.'

(I wished that people would stop commenting on my understanding of stuff.)

'Is Dad there?'

'No. He's asleep too.'

'Okay. When they wake up, could you tell them I'm okay?'

'Sure. Anyway, for your information, you're going to be in soooo much trouble, Jacob, when you get back. I swear.'

She said this like it was the best thing ever. I could *hear* her smile.

'Why?'

'You lost your phone, right? And Dad knows you missed the connecting flight. He's major moody.'

'It was snowing.'

'Oh. Okay. It's just that we checked departures. Your plane seemed to leave the airport fine.'

(When she said 'we', I knew she meant 'I'. She'd probably run downstairs with her phone to gleefully show Mum and Dad.)

'Well, I'm at an airport now and I'll be getting to LA today, so everything's on schedule.'

'Right. Weren't you meant to be in Hollywood on Tuesday? Today's Thursday?'

'Not in America, it's not. Just tell Mum and Dad that I'm in Albuquerque, getting a plane, and it's all legit.'

'Albu-what-que?'

I put the phone down without saying goodbye. I can be cold when necessary.

CHAPTER 24

Security

I saw his hat first. All cowboy-y and black. He sat with his back to us, just before the metal detectors.

I grabbed Jennifer before doing any further thinking. She was always good with plans. She stopped, forehead collapsing in wrinkles.

'What?'

I pointed. She saw.

'It's only . . .' she began. But she couldn't explain it away as only another hat. This was *the* hat. And that same ice-white hair cut round BFG ears.

He'd found us again.

(But how come he wasn't doing anything? It was creepy. Maybe he'd had a heart attack? Maybe he'd fallen asleep? Grandad was always drifting off in the afternoon.)

Up ahead, at security, a pair of uniforms looked scarily like cops. One stood behind a conveyor, waiting to pass trays through the scanner. The other stood past the grey plastic of the metal detector. Neither looked particularly scary, but still – we *were* fugitives from the law. And the two security officials *were* looking straight at us. But that was because it was late and there was hardly anyone else around, right? Dealing with us would probably make their evening less boring. Something to do to stay awake.

'Hey, what about the ashes?' I said. 'Will they let them through?'

'Why wouldn't they?'

'Because it's a dead person. No offence.'

But Jennifer was looking over her shoulder and Jennifer was swearing. If I ever introduced her to my parents, I'd have to warn them about her language. I could say it was an American thing and that she was older, like pretty much an adult.

What she'd seen, behind us and clear in the centre of the corridor, were two *actual* police officers. They stood. The odd tired family of tourists dribbled past them like a summer stream round a rock. The police were doing a bad job of acting naturally, especially since their uniform looked more like something a soldier would wear – all black with old-style caps and loads of gold detail. Whoever designed the clothes didn't want you mistaking these cops for the type that rescue kittens from trees.

And then I saw it: an emergency exit. A possible window (door) of opportunity. Illuminated by a spotlight straight from heaven pretty much. It was past security, okay. But if we sprinted through the metal detectors, I'm sure we could reach it before the yawning guards could react.

It opened with a push bar and there was a red exit sign above it. There was also a yellow poster, stuck underneath the push bar, with the words EMERGENCY EXIT. Across the door were two red fabric strips, the same sort used to organise queues. On the strips was written FIRE EXIT ONLY.

In short, it wasn't a door designed to be casually walked through.

'It's nothing,' said Jennifer. 'Maybe the Cowboy's going home. Maybe the police are patrolling. LA's so close, I can smell the smog. Don't let Miss Gonzalez's sacrifice be for nothing, Jay.'

She continued forward. We arrived at a stack of plastic

trays. At no point did anyone stop us. Maybe Jennifer was right. Maybe it *was* all coincidence. Because, thinking about it, there was nothing surprising about cops being in an airport.

Somewhere a child cried.

'Hold this,' said Jennifer and handed over the plastic bag.

She pulled our boarding passes from her back pocket and checked the details. As she did so, her hand trembled. I asked if she was all right.

'Fine,' she said, adding, 'I don't like flying and our seats aren't together.'

I was about to do a 'well, actually' about how statistically flying was safer than driving but an amplified voice bounced around the space like a toddler in a shopping trolley.

'Would Miss Gonzalez please make herself known to the closest official? We have some news regarding your ticket.'

Jennifer rolled her eyes.

'Maybe it's an upgrade?' I said.

'Yeah. Like that's going to happen.'

As she spoke, an avalanche of action kicked off:

1. The Cowboy yells, 'Grab the bag'.
2. Four more police officers rise around the X-Ray machine as if they'd been hiding underneath it.
3. Jennifer hisses, 'No!' like she has a puncture.
4. The child stops crying.

I'd learnt my lesson, however. I'd identified an escape route. And as long as I was never arrested, I could never get in trouble.

I spun Jennifer away as the cops dived at the space where she'd been standing. They missed like disorientated wrestlers. We darted through the metal detector. It didn't go off. Its guard grabbed at Jennifer's braids, but caught only air.

I heard shouted threats, as I pushed the emergency exit. The alarm was instant and teeth-shatteringly loud. I held the door as Jennifer ducked under the top tape and stepped over the bottom. With the police so close that we could smell their sweat, I followed her through, the door swinging shut behind us.

'Gulp,' I said, actually articulating the word.

At the top of a gloomy stairwell, steel steps like graph-paper lines zig-zagged down from our feet. Trouble rumbled behind us.

'Here goes nothing,' said Jennifer, descending, with me close behind.

Jennifer slammed through another door at the bottom and, although it was pretty much midnight, white light flooded the space.

We weren't *on* a runway. But immediately ahead *was* a plane. Probably ours and probably scheduled to shortly fly to LA, the front wheels bigger than a family car. Towering up high, the pilot sat flicking switches above his head. The engines roared warning. We took a sharp turn and ran round the thick supporting pillar that housed the stairs. In the shadows there was nothing to trip over but I still somehow managed to fall. And a proper dive too, like a striker on the losing team in the last minute of injury time.

I flew through the air, a tiny glider, instinctively letting go of the bag. As my palms met the American ground, scraping off British skin, the box hit the tarmac and broke free from the plastic. It bounced once, twice, and its lid came undone. Out soared the urn. This struck the ground and cracked open like a split peanut.

'Mom!' said Jennifer

But what spilt weren't ashes.

CHAPTER 25

Cache

There were (at least) ten rolls of banknotes, all held by elastic bands like belts round dressing gowns. There was also a tiny black drawstring bag, in which you might keep jewellery. It was a cache kept in a safe hidden behind a framed picture. And, in an instant, the Cowboy's desperation to retrieve it made sense. This was nobody's mother. This was someone's secret stash.

Jennifer froze, mouth gaping. But with footsteps banging against the emergency steps, and loud enough to be heard over the plane, we needed to move.

'Jennifer!' I called.

Although she was standing next to me, she was lost somewhere else. Her mouth opened, but if she said anything I didn't hear it.

I scooped everything from the tarmac into the plastic bag. I grabbed Jennifer's good arm, and pulled us behind the staircase's exterior wall, just as we heard the police crash out on to the runway. A classic first-person shooter movement.

We crouched with our backs to the wall, our hearts not daring to beat. From the other side of the breeze blocks came the Cowboy's voice.

'Jennifer! Don't do this. We're talking real-life danger, honey.'

Another voice. 'There!' it shouted. 'Under the baggage truck! Let's go!'

The plane began a slow taxi away. As its engines ramped up to a roar, the air shimmered. You could see the bright faces of passengers through circular windows like spotlights. I looked to Jennifer. She was staring blankly into the urn bag.

'Okay?' I called over the colliding noise of the engine's continuing roar and the whine of the alarm. Jennifer lifted her head and focused past the silver perimeter fence and parking lot beyond. 'Jennifer?' Her head turned. Her eyes were smudged red. The plane had passed, the sound of its engines fading. 'I'm sorry I dropped it.'

'No,' she said, the word alone in the sudden quiet.

She looked years younger, primary-school age. I wanted to hug her. Without the plane the alarm was more like the airport's heartbeat, less urgent. She sucked at her bottom lip, like she always did, and then stood up, her back scraping against the wall.

I got up too. 'Maybe with some superglue . . .' I said.

'It's nothing but . . .' She slid back down to the floor with a sigh, as if her legs were too upset to support her. 'I thought I was doing the right thing.'

Any reply caught in my throat. I nodded.

Dropping, I shuffled towards her. As our shoulders touched, I stretched an arm up and across. Because it's the right thing to do, you know, when someone's upset. Even if they're a girl and you're a boy and you've just smashed their urn, which up until this point the girl had thought contained her mum's ashes.

'You see?' said Jennifer, slowly shaking her head. 'You can't trust anybody.'

I cleared my throat. 'You can trust me,' I said.

America stretched out ahead, like the future, and all the way to the studios of Los Angeles. But that didn't matter any more. Because I was here, in the now, next to my friend.

'I know,' said Jennifer.

'Maybe . . .' I began.

'At least we've got cash. Bills, I mean,' said Jennifer, speaking herself back to the present. Words tumbled. 'And I'm going to be in so much trouble, by the way. Like if I wasn't already.' We looked at each other. Even in the runway's half-light, I could see the dark shadows under her eyes. 'So,' she said and punched my shoulder playfully.

I should tell her to stop doing this. I didn't flinch, even though it hurt again. Superhuman discipline.

'There'll be an army after us in thirty seconds. Are you good to go?' I asked, sounding like someone else, my more decisive imaginary older brother maybe.

'I'm good to go,' said Jennifer. 'With you.'

I made a sound like 'gah' but, luckily, she didn't seem to hear.

'What's in the black bag, by the way?'

I pulled it out. I opened its neck. Gently I shook the contents into my palm. Diamonds. I think. Their sparkle was like the life returning to Jennifer's eyes.

'Savage,' she said. 'What did I say about Lex Luthor?'

'Totally.'

In the shade under the airport gate we stood. Jennifer's smile may have wobbled a bit. And maybe mine did too. But, and here's the thing: we weren't finished yet.

The stairwell was an elephant leg supporting the long tubular body of gates above. I led her beneath the structure and through the shadows to the next supporting leg. Here was another door, just like the one we'd tumbled from.

We stepped through into a stairwell and climbed the metal steps as silently as we could. We eventually came to another door, which we pushed through. Automatic lights flicked on.

A new alarm sounded, and, if you can believe it, louder than the last. Even if it hadn't been blaring, the room rumbled with the rattle of machinery, the sort to shake your bones, enough to give you a migraine. The space was full of the kind of mad structure I used to make with Lego. Towers and racks and tracks all carrying speeding luggage.

'I've got an idea,' shouted Jennifer into my ear. 'How about you help me grab a bag?'

I didn't really have a choice. Jennifer had only the one fully functioning arm and, as you know, I'm, like, stupidly polite. So I helped and we thudded a suitcase to the floor.

Jennifer fell to her knees and unzipped the suitcase, flopping it open like she was turning a heavy page of a massive book. She studied its contents and then looked up. Her smile didn't fill me with confidence.

'Maybe not the disguise I was thinking.'

On top of a pile of brightly coloured clothes sat an oversized bow tie and a green wig. I thought back to the group in McDonald's. This was their kit.

She tried another bag. More clown clothes.

'There's no time to go through every suitcase. And, thinking about it, it's perfect.'

'No way,' I shouted. Like, pretty much, an actual shout. 'I'm not doing it. I don't want to look like an idiot. Here's where I draw the line.'

CHAPTER 26

Recreational Vehicle

Dressed as clowns and out of breath, we ran into the airport car park.

Screaming brakes and an exploding horn. And the sounds combined to tear gashes from the air. To Jennifer's right, kissing distance from her cheek, a huge white motorhome had stopped. A thick roof folded over the front windscreen like a quiff. Three people sat in its cab and, as it braked, they jerked forward and back.

Jennifer still had her sling, made from the Oklahoma state trooper's bandana. Now she also wore trousers, or pants, matching her waistcoat and patterned with a headache-inducing green, blue and red check. Her jacket had long tails and one side was coloured red and the other blue. At the collar of her white shirt was a multicoloured bow tie secured with elastic. Naturally she had a huge red nose and a huger red wig that sat on her head like the round foliage of a cartoon tree.

Me? I'd pulled on a white satin top over my own (sweaty) T-shirt. It was decorated with two weird collars that ruffled two red rings round my neck. Three fluffy balls formed a line down my front. I guess these were meant to look like buttons. My trousers were made of the same white satin as my top and were so flimsy and huge I'd pulled them on over my jeans because the alternative would have been disturbing. I didn't have a wig but, instead, wore a bit of plastic that covered my head and, if I'd taken any time to put it on properly, might have made it look as if I were going bald. Two clumps of blue 'hair' sat above my ears. The finishing touch was the red satin cape that hung from my shoulders and almost touched my ankles.

Yes, a cape.

Now, usually in this situation you might expect the driver to be shaking a tight fist of knuckles, especially in America.

'What are you doing, you clowns?' he might have shouted.

But, under his black baseball cap with a capital B, this

driver smiled and offered a thumbs up. Alongside him two passengers joined in the smiling. One, bald and red-faced, also waved, and the other, a tiny woman with big hair, did an okay symbol with one hand. With the other she took a picture of us on her phone.

Jennifer shrugged. 'Could we catch a ride, sir?' she asked, miming her request with her good hand, pointing at me and her and then the motorhome. She spoke quickly because she knew that, at any time, the Cowboy was likely to come tumbling into the car park. The longer we stood here, the less likely things would turn out okay.

The driver wound down his side window and poked out his head.

'Have we met before?' he asked.

Jennifer looked at me. Of all the responses I wasn't expecting that one. I tightened my grip of the urn bag, ready for something bad to happen. Because this was weird. And, like, weirder than all the other weird stuff that had happened already, which itself had all been pretty weird.

'Don't think so,' she said. 'Maybe it was another clown?'

The driver turned to his friends. We couldn't hear what they whispered. There was much gesticulation but also plenty of nodding.

'We three, we just love clowns,' said the driver, head out of the window again. 'Where you headed?'

'LA,' exploded Jennifer, jumping closer to the vehicle, glancing over her shoulder. 'For a clown expo. We can give you money for gas.'

The driver's friends nodded heads and gave two thumbs up each.

'The name's Ray but my friends call me John. We're travelling to Vegas,' said the driver. The bald guy hissed at him. 'On vacation,' said the driver quickly and in a really weird way that could only mean they weren't. 'That's on the way, right? Get in the back. The more, the merrier. It's not every day you almost run over a clown.'

Jennifer thanked him (I did too, but nobody heard) and pulled open the rear door. It was right next to the driver's and thin and plastic and something like you'd have on a caravan.

'What's the worst that could happen?' she said and stepped out of view.

Once again there was nothing to do but follow. I clambered after her, falling into the RV and on to her lap as the motor jolted forward.

'My wrist!' she said as I struggled free.

'Sorry.'

181

I leant across to close the door, which swung at the side of the vehicle like an elephant's ear. As it closed, it trapped us in with a sudden strange smell. Something like flowers. But overripe flowers. Nice but overpowering, like your gran's perfume. There was no time for sniffing, however – we were being watched. The two not driving craned their necks to nod and smile like bad actors at a wedding.

'What're your names, friends?' asked the bald man. 'I'm Richard. My friend here is Mary. You've met Ray.'

'John,' said Ray/John. 'I prefer John.'

'Jennifer,' I said. 'And Jacob.'

'Who's who?' asked Richard. I opened my mouth to answer. 'I'm kidding, I'm kidding.' Without pausing he continued: 'You ever read Charles Fort, Jacob?' I hadn't. '"We shall pick up an existence by its frogs!"'

He waited for a reaction that never came. Mainly because I had absolutely no idea what he was talking about.

The driver spoke, rescuing me from the potentially eternal awkwardness.

'Embrace coincidence! Accept the weird! Allow synchronicity! That's what Richard means,' he said. 'Oh, and belt up!'

'Who's Charles Fort?' asked Jennifer and as the driver explained that Charles Fort lived a hundred years ago and wrote about weird phenomena, I wondered whether it would be better to be out being chased or in with the Forteans.

'Hell, we sure like the bizarre,' said the driver.

As we reached for our seat belts, I visualised the Cowboy, who, at this very moment, was surely moseying into the car park. And no doubt he watched the motorhome career into the New Mexico night. And no doubt he made a note of the registration plate. And, most def, he lit another cigarette and hatched another plan.

PART 3

THURSDAY

★ ★ ★
TIME UNTIL THE MOVIE SHOOT:
11 HOURS 13 MINUTES

CHAPTER 27

I Want to Believe

We were on Interstate 40. I knew this by the little roadside red and blue shields the headlights picked out every so often. We'd left Albuquerque airport with no trouble. A high-speed chase between a motorhome and half a dozen police cars might have been fun, but it wasn't to be, not tonight. And, anyway, that sort of thing is probably more enjoyable to watch than be part of.

Jennifer chatted as I took in the RV's strange interior. There was a huge poster occupying most of the wall directly in front of us. A flying saucer hovered over trees and the phrase 'I want to believe'. There were half a dozen copies of a magazine called *Fortean Times* on a small table.

You might think I felt creeped out, threatened even, by the driver and his two friends. But it would take something special to be more threatening than the Cowboy, with his manner, moustache and matiness with local law enforcement.

'Why were you in Albuquerque?' asked Jennifer.

It was an innocent, simple question. All three answered at once, though, and quickly.

'Sightseeing,' said John.

'Business,' said Richard.

'Big . . . fishing?' said Mary, not convincing even herself.

I know Jennifer wanted to catch my glance in order to roll her eyes, but I pretended I was lost in thought, doing some deep contemplation like a proper adult. I was soooo tired, sitting strapped into the sofa, my arm stretched across the top of its cushioned back, away from Jennifer. I stared vacantly through the thick plastic window, a bubble from the side of the vehicle. Was it desert outside? That darkness past the dull glow of the road? It wasn't hot, but maybe this was down to the air conditioner being set to freezing. I missed my stolen coat. The flimsy clown shirt was as effective as tissue paper in keeping me warm.

(Our wigs sat abandoned like dead pets on the motorhome's thin carpet. We were now only two-thirds clown.)

I tried to zone out, to clear my mind and exist in the moment, like the YouTube clips in wellbeing lessons say to do. At moments like this, when me and Jennifer weren't rushing about, it was difficult to escape a feeling of creeping dread like I was slowly being covered by a blanket of PANIC. A PANIC blanket.

'Have you heard of Area fifty-one?' asked John, the driver. It's hard to feel mindful when forced to listen to conspiracy theories. 'It's an air force facility in Nevada. They store, examine and reverse-engineer technologies rescued from crashed extra-terrestrial spacecraft. Roswell, for instance.'

'Ros-what?' asked Jennifer.

'Roswell, New Mexico. The first documented crash landing of an alien craft. Bodies were recovered.'

'Okaaaaay,' said Jennifer.

I made a mental note to tell her later about the dad of a kid in the year below who'd fallen off his bike and had woken up believing the world to be flat.

'Kevlar, the heat-resistant material. Fibre optics, night vision, laser cutting, the integrated chip: all "discovered" after Roswell.'

Richard sighed theatrically.

'What?' said John.

'You're talking too much.'

'And the problem is? You think Bozo and her friend are with "them"? They're clowns! No offence.'

'Trust nobody,' said Richard. He had a nasal voice and I was coming to the decision that I didn't like him. 'And especially when they're dressed as clowns.'

'Amen to that,' said Mary.

Jennifer puffed out her cheeks. 'Well,' she said. 'Thanks for the lift, anyway. I never knew conspiracy theorists could be so nice.'

The RV screeched to a halt, throwing me into Jennifer. The furniture shifted with a noise that sounded like a groan. It was a good job there wasn't anyone directly behind us or we'd have been in a pile-up.

The three up front turned their bodies and craned their necks to face us. It didn't look very comfortable. Their mouths were zigzags of anger.

'We're no conspiracy theorists,' said John from under his cap, in a voice like a puppy growling.

'We prefer the nomenclature "ufologists",' said Richard. He pronounced it 'u-follow-jists'.

'And we *are* nice,' said Mary. '*So* nice.'

'Too nice,' said Richard. 'I'm always saying. Aren't I always?'

'Sorry,' said Jennifer, obviously worried that we were about to get thrown out. 'I didn't realise.'

The three turned back to the windscreen.

'No problem,' said John, shifting the gear into drive, voice light and carefree. 'It's one of those things.'

The RV shuddered back into motion. Jennifer wide-eyed me, motioning with her good hand like I should say something. I cleared my throat.

'I saw some weird lights in the sky once.'

Now Jennifer side-eyed me. Could I do anything right?

'Tell us,' said Richard, turning again, like I'd said I had a bucket of KFC going free.

'Do you mind if I record you?' said Mary, her phone already raised. 'For documentary purposes.'

I shrugged. 'Well . . .'

Should I make something up? My story wasn't great. It didn't deserve to be recorded.

'It was a dark and stormy night. My phone had stopped working. But it had probably run out of charge. There was an eerie electric feel to the air.'

'Classic signs,' said Mary.

Richard shushed her.

'And I looked out of my bedroom window and I saw

this crazy triangle of lights in the sky, kind of moving in and out of the clouds.'

I made the mistake of catching Jennifer's eye. Her lips wobbled in a kind of foreshock before the main laughter earthquake.

'Carry on,' said Richard.

'Lovin' it,' said John.

I spoke quietly. 'It turned out to be an EasyJet flight to Malaga. Mum has this app where you—'

Laughter exploded from Jennifer like a geyser. Instantly she covered her mouth with her good hand. 'I'm so sorry,' she said.

Richard spoke like he hadn't heard her.

'It's not unknown for crafts of extra-terrestrial origin to disguise themselves as commercial aircraft,' said Richard. 'For your information.'

This wasn't a conversation I wanted to get trapped in, so I tried changing topic.

'How far from California are we?' I asked, turning to Jennifer, dismissing all thoughts of aliens and mindfulness. She frowned. 'A distance, right?'

My insides danced with painful energy. They knew the answer already.

'Like a loooong way,' said Jennifer. 'Like seeeeeven

hundred miles.' Then she realised why I'd asked: my scene was shooting at noon. Today. 'Oh.' She leant across, putting an arm round my shoulder. I shook my head, looked to my lap. If we'd taken a train, we'd have maybe made it. If we'd flown, we'd have got there in the morning. Now that we were driving . . . 'But we can still do it.' She called to John. 'How long to Vegas?'

'Nine hours,' he said. 'Eight, maybe.'

'And how far's Hollywood from there?'

'A distance. Maybe four hours if you're driving. Now, if you had a craft propelled by gravity control, you're talking minutes.'

Richard and Mary grunted agreement.

(It was about two in the morning. Eight plus four is twelve. Minus the time difference that meant one in the afternoon arrival time. And that's if everything went smoothly, which wasn't my experience of America. We'd arrive late, but close enough to make missing the scene all the more needlingly painful.)

'Oh,' said Jennifer in a very un-Jennifer way. 'And they definitely said midday?'

She wasn't even persuading herself. Because there's no cheating the ticking of time. Clocks won't do you favours.

'It doesn't matter. It's only a stupid film. It would've been lame anyway. Like Doctor Bong or someone.'

(Doctor Bong is a superhero with a bell for a head. He can make things happen by bonging. He's not great.)

'Is everything okay?' asked John, glancing in the rear-view mirror.

'Did someone say bong?' asked Mary.

Jennifer rubbed my back as I leant forward, head in hands, but otherwise taking it like a legend.

'Jay was meant to be in a movie,' she said. 'Today.'

'Was it a clown movie?' asked John, grinning like an idiot. 'At the clown expo?'

'Superhero,' I said. 'A superhero movie.'

'Sorry, hon, even with the time difference, you're not going to make it.'

I'd failed. I wasn't getting to Hollywood on time. People talk about dreams coming true all the time. And they mean stupid stuff like a takeaway pizza or their football team scoring. I'd won a competition to appear in a superhero movie. And I never win anything. It was literally a dream come true, a once-in-a-lifetime event.

But, you know what, catching a lift across Arizona with UFO nuts, being pursued by a US marshal (retired) and doing it all alongside the most kick-ass person I'd ever met (and one with a plastic bag full of tens of thousands of dollars), I was kind of enjoying myself in a way I never really had before.

'It sucks,' said Jennifer. 'Really. But, y'know, it's not over till it's over. Road trips never work out the way you think they will. That's their second rule.'

'What's the first?'

'You don't talk about what happened on them.'

'Right.'

We laughed. A connection. That diamond sparkle of her eyes. Maybe I should move to the States? Like permanently. People do. I could tour Hollywood when I was older. I could become a world-famous actor and star in superhero films then too. I'd have a Hollywood house with a swimming pool, one of those ones where the water level matches the horizon. It was fiiiine. In America anything is possible.

(And child actors *always* get messed up and never make it big, anyway, so—)

Doctor Bong, Doctor Bong, I kept thinking. *Only Doctor Bong.*

How I was going to break all this to my parents I had no idea.

CHAPTER 28

Hard Sell
Outside Kingman, Arizona

Thursday sunrise and in the back of the speeding mobile home, Jennifer's mouth gaped. She did that thing where her head dropped and the movement woke her and she'd lift her chin and then eventually it would drop again and again and again.

I sat there feeling dirty. Unclean, I mean. My hair was greasy, my scalp itchy. Never in my life had I so wanted a shower. Mum would have been proud.

A man with an English accent spoke about the 'Manises UFO incident'. It was a podcast and I swear the presenter said 'or was it?' after every statement he made about how this UFO was probably lights from a local factory or Venus or whatever.

Or was it?

I must have fallen back asleep because suddenly the RV had stopped and the cab was empty and there was no voice talking about extra-terrestrial visitors. The sky was definitely lighter. What was happening? Had the ufologists been abducted?

'Coffee stop,' said John, standing outside at the open living-space door like he'd teleported there. 'Gooood morning to you both. What a day for it.'

I shook Jennifer's shoulder. There was no gradual coming to for her, no moment of confusion – as soon as her eyes opened, she unbuckled and was up and out, holding the urn bag close to her chest. I followed her, my head feeling like it was stuffed with fluffy sheep.

I was expecting to step into an American version of a service station or, at least, one of the food courts I'd already visited over here. (Could I manage another burger? For breakfast? Duh, of course.) Instead we were greeted by a huge sign that read ARMCO GAS in stylised white lettering.

'Arizona,' said Jennifer. 'This is as fun as it gets around here.'

'It looks like a Western,' I said, taking in the morning of sand-coloured dust and odd clumps of balding grass, and immediately wished I hadn't because it reminded us of the Cowboy on our trail.

'Ten minutes and return to the road?' asked John like we were on a school trip. A breeze whipped at his cap. 'And if you want to be eating, there are better places in Vegas.'

Already his two mates were walking towards the single-storey brick building that, alongside petrol pumps and a couple of white Armco Gas tanks, was the only thing here and maybe even in the rest of Arizona. Mary was taking pictures. Richard was grumbling.

Jennifer held back until they'd disappeared inside, an old-style bell ringing as they passed through. She turned. And, as she looked me up and down, she stifled a laugh.

'What?'

But I knew what.

I pulled off my clown top and threw it to the floor. Feeble dust clouds rose. And I took off my trousers and chucked these too, just about keeping my balance as I pulled them over my trainers. And, with this top layer off, I wouldn't say I was warm but it *was* defo hotter here. About the same temperature as a disappointing summer's day in Somerset.

'You're going to need to bring those with you,' she said.

'Why?'

Okay, so there was a fleck of anger to my voice. She *always* knew best.

'Partly not to be traced, bae. But mostly because it's littering and you might get a fine. But, you know, totally up to you.'

I scooped the satin from the Arizonan dirt, muttering how nobody likes a know-it-all.

She held up the bag. The broken edges of the urn pushed against the plastic. I shoved in the clown clothes. She kept hers on.

'We can get some new threads here,' she said. 'We're rich, remember. Gucci, baby!'

'About that . . .'

'An advance on my inheritance. It's what Mom would have wanted.'

Inside was like a museum shop. Jennifer was straight over to the hoodies and jumpers that had 'Navajo Nation' splashed across them. She asked what colour I wanted. I said blue. She said not to be so predictable. I wandered away to study shelves of 'genuine' arrows.

I felt a presence at my shoulder. I lifted an arrow. It could do some damage, whistling through the air. The thing about guns is they're so loud. I'd hate to be hit by an arrow, silent like a gas leak.

'How about we get this? There are no bows, so you'd just have to jab people with it.'

I did some air-jabbing. It felt satisfying.

'We sell bows too, friend. Good morning to you. And a mighty fine morning it is too. You ever get that feeling that it's going to be a great day?' It wasn't Jennifer. It was a man with a pink face like he'd been out in the sun too long. He was wearing a green polo shirt with a badge that said DAVE. He was also sniffing at the air. 'Like you could almost smell it?'

I put the arrow back. 'Yep,' I said. 'Anyway. Sorry.'

'We have guns too.' Dave leant into me. His nose almost touched mine. One thing I could smell was his breath. It smelt of coffee, and faintly of alcohol. 'But you're probably too young for all that. He straightened his back. 'How old are you?'

'Too young.'

Dave smiled, revealing teeth that looked like they'd been carved from ivory.

'You want to see something super sweet? Follow me.'

We walked a line of shelves and came to a jewellery display. He lifted a necklace. It was a black string with a tiny silver horse attached to it.

'You've got a sweetheart, right? A handsome kid like

you. Lucky son of a . . .' His voice faded. Briefly he seemed lost. 'I'll tell you what. She'd love you for this. Or he. It's 2019. Anyhow, it's a good-luck charm. Who doesn't like good luck? Am I right?'

A card price tag hung from it. $150. I pointed at some fabric wristbands.

'What about them?'

'Friendship bracelets,' said Dave. 'For kids. You're no kid. I can see that by the way you hold yourself. Straight back. Proud shoulders. Tell you what, maybe we could discuss a deal on that good-luck pendant? A discount between buddies.'

Jennifer appeared with a (new) plastic bag – she'd obviously already paid.

'What's going on?' she asked, face set to full sass.

'This man—'

Dave interrupted. 'The name's Dave.'

Jennifer looked confused.

'I'm Dave,' he confirmed.

I couldn't work out whether he was being polite or PO'd. His voice was weirdly without tone.

'Dave's showing me good-luck charms. Expensive ones.'

'You can't put a price on good luck,' he said. 'That's

what Mother Dave always used to say. They allow jewellery in the circus, sweetheart?'

Jennifer swept her headlight eyes from me to Dave.

'Please don't call me sweetheart,' she said. 'It's creepy. We're going, Jacob.'

She swung the two bags she held in her good hand. I'm not sure she meant to hit me between the legs, but she did. I let out air with a sound like 'ooof'.

Dave sniggered and Jennifer, rolling her eyes, sighed like *I* was the problem.

'Have a great one,' called Dave from behind us. 'Good luck!'

'Don't they have stores in England?' said Jennifer as we left. 'You never been in a store before?'

CHAPTER 29

Jumpers

Outside, the morning sun's welcoming sting briefly distracted me from the dull ache of my testicles.

'That really hurt,' I said as we headed for the alien motorhome.

'Serves you right. The way you fell for the sales patter.'

Jennifer slapped the new plastic bag into my chest. She said to quit complaining and get the sweatshirt on. She'd bought a purple one, thinking the colour would suit me. (I don't think she was being serious.)

'There's chips and soda too. I didn't want to be eating nutrition pills or whatever space crap UFO bros have. Don't let the Advil fall out.'

As I pulled my head through the purple fabric, I said that I'd never really been a jumper person.

'I'm sorry? A what?'

'A jumper person.'

She stared like I'd stopped talking and had started making honking noises.

'What's that supposed to mean? Like kangaroos?'

'No. Jumper. Like sweatshirts. Jumpers.'

'Honestly, Jacob, sometimes it's like you're speaking a different language.'

This was probably an opportunity to say something funny but I was too busy staring slack-jawed and pointing an electric finger at a pick-up truck parked at the far end of the lot. It hadn't been there when we'd arrived, I was sure.

'The Cowboy,' I said.

'It's a pick-up.'

'Yeah. It's *his* pick-up. I saw it in Catoosa.'

'Don't worry,' she said. 'The country's full of pick-ups like that. Seriously.'

She didn't sound convincing.

John and his two friends were already at the RV and motioning for us to hurry like we were late, which we weren't. But wanting to leave as quickly as possible, I broke into a little jog. I was all strapped up and ready to go by the time Jennifer clambered in.

There was a different smell now. John, Richard and Mary turned to us, chewing open-mouthed. Their lips and tongues and teeth made a disgusting smacking sound. Mary offered a package: DRIED BUFFALO MEAT. Jennifer was busy straightening out her sling, so I turned down the offer on her behalf.

And then John said, 'You've got to be kidding me,' and not because he'd realised what he was eating. There was a problem starting the engine. Richard and Mary each leant across to try the ignition themselves. It didn't work. They pushed buttons. The hazard lights flashed. The horn sounded. They moved the gear selector. But nothing made any difference. The motorhome wouldn't stir.

'Houston, we have a problem,' said John to us, his eyebrows a metre above his head, way past the baseball cap.

'Engines don't just stop working,' said Richard.

Mary was pointing at the roof to suggest, I guess, that aliens had a hand (flipper? claw?) in the trouble.

John stumbled out. His two friends followed. The front windscreen was full of bonnet as they tried to work a solution.

'Of all the people. Of all the cars. We had to get these

clowns,' hissed Jennifer. We both looked at the wigs on the floor. 'Okay, okay, I know, I know.' She stood up. 'Let's get changed. In case we need to make a quick getaway.'

'I thought you said—'

She cut me off. 'Give me a hand.'

Next on the menu was massive awkwardness. I helped pull off her clown top. She was wearing a white T-shirt underneath.

'So your wrist's no better?' I said because I was bursting to speak.

'Not when you're knocking it. Focus, Jay.'

I helped the jumper over her head. I looked everywhere but her.

'We so need to find a shower in Vegas,' she said. 'Like, dive in for five seconds. Boom. Surgical strike.'

(Could she smell me? Did I smell bad? I mean, it wasn't as if I could ask.)

I guided her 'bad' hand through the sleeve, as quickly as I could. She winced for my benefit, I'm sure. If she didn't catch up with her dad in LA, she could always try acting.

I didn't try speaking again because I knew my voice would be helium high. I'd learnt never to trust my body.

It was always waiting for an opportunity to make me look like an idiot.

'You need to tie this round my neck,' she said, meaning the sling. She moved her hair aside with her good hand. I found myself staring at the nape of her neck and I'm not sure why. 'What are you waiting for?' she asked.

My fingers jumped to fumbling with the fabric, twisting it this way and that.

What started as innocently helping out a criminal on the run was now turning weird and heavy. But all things pass, even Maths lessons, and it was done soon enough. She turned round, her arm safely in the bandana.

She smiled, our mouths not more than fifteen centimetres away. Her nose was scrunched up. I remember noticing that as the RV's engine coughed into life, making me jump, sending shivers through the air.

She looked over my shoulder as I disappeared into a sinkhole of disappointment. The ufologists were getting back in.

'What was wrong?' she asked. 'How'd you get it started?'

The UFO people didn't reply but took their seats in silence. It was weird. Something was definitely up. And I had this stone-in-the-stomach feeling that it wasn't extra-terrestrial. I *think* Jennifer sighed at me, but the noise might have come from the door opening and . . .

There, bowing slightly to inspect the space like a vulture dropping its head at a dead coyote, was the Cowboy.

'It *was* his pick-up!' I said, and hated myself.

'Howdy,' said the Cowboy, because, of course, he would say that. 'Hope I'm not interrupting anything.'

He had an unlit cigarette hanging from the corner of his mouth. His caterpillar moustache looked whiter than ever, as colourless as an empty canvas.

'Hi,' I said, my voice wobbling only slightly.

Jennifer was glaring. Both at me and the Cowboy. Back and forth with the glare, like a furious tennis match.

'I helped our friends here with their little engine trouble. They'll be on their way shortly. Without you two, suffice to say.'

'We're not coming,' said Jennifer. 'You can't force us.'

As the Cowboy smiled, his perfect teeth twinkled.

'I'd be happy to contact local law enforcement again, if that's what it takes.' Jennifer shrugged. 'Or your grandmother. Would you like to speak to her?'

I felt like I should be asking 'What about me?' but instead I stood there like a melt.

It would be great to be as tall as this cowboy but nowhere near as great as being on a plane to LA, I thought. *With Jennifer. Drinking a Coke. Sharing Haribo. The lot.*

'Y'know, in the past, back when I was in the marshal service, I've told you about that, right?' asked the Cowboy. I nodded. 'When I caught up with them, the people I hunted, because I always did catch them, and that's no idle boast, that's a statement of fact, when I caught up with them, I'd always say, "It's nothing personal; it's my job." Here's the thing, see: I lied. Didn't know it back then, but I've had time to think recently. It *was* personal. It was me against them, that's why. And when I was a young man, I liked to win. I got satisfaction from it. Childish, really. Now, you two, you've caused more trouble than I like to remember. But . . . it's nothing personal. And I mean that with all my heart. So come along and we'll straighten things out. You hungry? I bet you are. How about pancakes?'

My stomach rumbled, the selfish turncoat organ.

'No,' said Jennifer. I glanced over. Because, I mean, it wasn't 100 per cent clear what she was saying no to. 'We're not coming.'

'Right,' I said, but quietly.

'Young woman, you and me both know who I'm

working for. And you and me both know that she don't take disappointment lightly.' He studied us like a fox does a pet rabbit. 'I've not smoked in five years. Now look what you've done. Coughing every twenty minutes. How's the wrist?'

Jennifer shook her head. 'What do you care?'

I felt like I should say something in her defence.

'She has it in a sling,' I said. 'So . . .'

I wanted to appear helpful, like a hostage negotiator. I ended up sounding sarcastic. Which Jennifer loved, laughing.

The Cowboy was less of a fan. He pushed his hat back from his forehead and had this expression like he'd swallowed a stick of dynamite.

'Where's the package?' he asked, voice gun-barrel hard. 'The jig is up.'

It wasn't necessarily me that gave it away. Jennifer, she might have really obviously looked at the urn bag on the floor as well. When she said, 'We lost it,' she was fooling nobody and she knew it. So much so that as the Cowboy went to step up into the cabin, she dived fully into the front seats. From standing to a full-on Superman leap. A gymnastic wonder.

The Cowboy paused, ruefully shaking his head as he

watched her land on the laps up top. 'Really?' he asked. 'Ain't we had plenty enough fun already?'

Whatever he'd said to John/Richard/Mary had them frozen. Even with a teenager banging about on their bodies.

'Hey,' dared Richard.

The other two kept silent.

'Sorry,' I said, scooping the urn bag from the floor.

And, as I did so, the RV started to roll backwards.

CHAPTER 30

Gas

Me and the Cowboy realised what was happening at the same time. We even caught each other's eye. As he tried stepping up into the RV, his hands grabbing at the door frame, I tried reaching Jennifer. Because she'd managed, and I don't know how, to release the parking brake.

Her legs and the arms of the UFO people moved everywhere, like a cartoon brawl. Without the brake on the motorhome moved backwards, picking up speed. And we must have hit a pothole or something. Whatever it was, the bump threw me and the Cowboy down – only I was inside and he wasn't.

'Umph,' I heard him say as the air was knocked from his chest.

There was loads of shouting and most of it swearing,

especially as Jennifer's legs and knees hit people's groins. I kept a tight grip on the bag.

'What are you doing?'

'Get off my pants!'

'Are you crazy, girlfriend?'

The RV bunny-hopped into sudden speed, the engine coughing complaint as we picked up momentum.

Did someone have a foot on the pedal? I was struck down again, just as I glimpsed six hands on the steering wheel. I hit my head on the edge of the sofa with a sharp thwack.

The side door flapped as the RV bounced backwards over the bumpy ground, plastic creaking. Before I realised what we were headed towards, I was relieved, at least, that we'd not run over the Cowboy. That would have been *properly* bad.

'Oh, mother of mercy, have pity on me,' said Richard as some dried buffalo meat smacked me in the face.

I grabbed at the edge of the sofa, my underpowered biceps shuddering to pull me up. Through the two square rear windows, a tall white gas container loomed impossibly large and suicidally close. And still the engine whined.

'Jennifer!' I shouted, the view filling with appalling

white. I'd played enough video games to know that hitting gas tanks was best avoided.

The back of the RV rose as we hit the dirt incline, put there to protect the gas. I fell once again, rolling until I struck the partition between the living space and the cab.

There was a huge smash, and a part ripping, part screaming of bent metal. And we stopped. There was no explosion. There was no fire. There *was* the Cowboy, though, without his hat, pulling open the door and ordering us out, veins bursting from his forehead. And there was also a raging hissing sound, a fire hose of whispers.

The gas.

I crawled out, still holding on to the bag, and dropped on to the mound of soil. I ate dirt and I rolled. But, made athletic by the possibility of death, I was soon up and sprinting. I joined Jennifer, the three ufologists and the Cowboy, as we flew towards Dave's store.

Three . . . two . . . one . . .

A monumental boom ripped across Arizona, sounding like every firework I'd ever heard exploding at once. It launched a wall of air rushing past our ears. A tidal wave of heat followed. I felt it first on the tips of my ears, and it took our legs from us and we were airborne. There was a roller-coaster adrenalin rush to the absence of gravity.

Until we landed. With a crunch of twisted ankles and bruised elbows.

And, once again, superpowers would have been handy.

A split second of complete silence extended as the universe held its breath. It broke with a cough. And then a moan. And Jennifer sat up and pointed. I followed the direction of her finger. Like a broken oil well, where there'd been a gas container, flames now blossomed into the cloudless sky around the RV, which was black and red with heat. You could feel it against your skin.

A voice spoke over the crackling fire. 'Are you from the government?' asked Mary, before breaking into a coughing fit.

The Cowboy stood. He pulled Jennifer up, then offered me a hand. Orange roared behind him.

'Something like that,' he said. 'Now where's my hat?'

CHAPTER 31

Fourteen Years
Route 93, Arizona

'**W**here are you taking us?' asked Jennifer eventually.

The cab stank of charcoal. The right side of my face felt like it was on fire. It wasn't, though. Both the Cowboy and Jennifer had checked – more than once. Maybe the sensation wasn't even down to the explosion. Maybe it was my body finally reacting to everything it has been through.

'West,' said the Cowboy.

The three of us sat shoulder to shoulder in the pick-up as it sped towards the horizon. Jennifer had the middle seat because the Cowboy couldn't trust her not to do something stupid like open the door at seventy-five miles an hour. For the first fifteen minutes we sat without talking, shocked into silence by the explosive events at the gas station. The singed urn bag was safely stowed in the space behind our seats. I was kind of happy not to have to worry about it any more.

'You know, you're just like your grandmother,' the Cowboy growled. He'd obviously spent this time shaking up his thoughts like a can of Coke. The pressure was now so great that they exploded from him. 'Impulsive. Too quick to make a decision. It'll get you in trouble one day, young lady. Real trouble guaranteed. You remember that.'

I let out a tired laugh. I couldn't help it. Because if *this* wasn't trouble, I didn't know what was.

The Cowboy had given the UFO gang a bunch of money from a briefcase pulled from the pick-up. It might not have made them feel any better but it sure stopped them crying about the RV. And they were totally convinced that he was a 'man in black'.

Dave was outside within seconds of the explosion. I'd never seen someone look so shocked. You know in cartoons when the character's jaw literally hits the ground? That's pretty much what happened with him. The Cowboy handed Dave cash too. He also whispered something into his ear, which broke his trance and, if you can believe it, made him smile.

'It was a good job that tank didn't have a line to the buildings or elsewhere. We'd have been as good as dead.'

'Yeah, okay, whatever, but where exactly west?' asked Jennifer, like she'd heard none of what the Cowboy had said.

'To Vegas,' he said. 'McCarran airport.'

I closed my eyes. If they thought I was asleep, they wouldn't include me. I didn't even care that I'd assumed we were driving to Chicago, back to Jennifer's family. Everywhere was a distance away. And everywhere was also unimaginably far from home. I'd missed the shoot, Jennifer had been caught, so what did anything matter any more?

'Yep, McCarran airport,' said the Cowboy again. 'That's where you're going. On a plane back to Illinois, school and your grandmother. And how about you, sonny? Do your parents know where you're at?' I let my mouth hang open, breathing heavily. It was top-grade acting, even though I could smell my breath and it made me desperate for a toothbrush. I didn't want to think about Mum and Dad. I didn't want to think about the inevitable call I'd have to make. 'I know you're not sleeping.'

Jennifer, who should have been my ally, elbowed me

in the side. I straightened up, the safety belt tightening across my chest, and rubbed my eyes.

'What?' I said, continuing with my show. 'Where am I?'

'Your parents?' said the Cowboy. 'What's their story?'

'They know,' I said, fake yawning. 'They're cool. I rang home yesterday. Thanks for asking.'

I'd tried to sound confident, but my voice had betrayed me with a wobble. The Cowboy laughed. It sounded like sandpaper on metal and soon turned into a cough. He pulled a bottle of water from a compartment near the gear selector and drank.

'You excuse me,' he said. 'Where was I? Yes, as soon as we get ourselves to Vegas, I'll be letting you ring them again to confirm all that coolness. And then I'm putting you on a plane and putting your friend Jennifer on one too and returning this here box to the boss. And then I'm done. Anyone want water?'

(We didn't.)

'Take it from me, you don't want to be making an enemy of your friend's grandmother here. Not if you ever plan on visiting the States again. Say I'm wrong, Jennifer.' But she said nothing. 'You may be fourteen, girl, but you're no fool, I can see that.'

'You're fourteen!' I hissed, this information shaking me from the dull truth that to live is to suffer and any plan I'd ever had to get to LA had *always* been destined to fail.

Jennifer looked down her nose and shrugged. 'I'm mature for my age.'

'But *I'm* fourteen. I thought you were, like, eighteen or something. Like an adult. You said you could drive. You had ID.'

'Fake ID. And I *can* drive. Just not legally.' Jennifer stared through the windscreen, out at the road as straight as an arrow. 'We're all pretending to be someone else anyway,' she said finally.

CHAPTER 32

What's Your Name?
Las Vegas, Nevada

'Used to be a big mafia town,' said the Cowboy. 'Some reckon it still is.'

The morning had raised a radioactive orange. We were on the outskirts of Vegas, heading in. Telegraph wires crossed the road like pencil marks against the sky. Huge trucks rumbled on to our road from massive spirals of tarmac. And we continued onwards, past palm trees outside car dealerships opening for another day of sweaty sales talk.

We passed a huge green rectangle that rose from the central reservation. It announced Sunset Road to be half a mile away, that Galleria Drive was three-quarters of a mile distant, and it was two miles to Russell Drive. These places meant something to somebody. People lived there. Maybe even fourteen-year-olds . . . like us.

'They say there's hundreds of bodies buried in the desert. It's not healthy to imagine it too vividly. Hell, there's nothing like the Las Vegas Expressway to get you down. If a mafioso offers to give you a lift home, you say no, you hear me? That's all I'm saying.'

He held the steering wheel with his huge leathery hands and he shook his head ruefully. Jennifer sat between us with a straight back. Her good hand was in her lap, her bad hand was in the sling. And if it wasn't for her eyes being shut, you'd have thought she was studying the rear of the tank-sized four-by-four up ahead and, in particular, the bumper sticker that said IF YOU CAN READ THIS, YOU'RE TOO FRICKING CLOSE. As it was, it looked as if she were meditating, her face perfectly at ease.

'You've been here before?' I asked the Cowboy, daring to chat, given confidence by the weird situation, feeling more like I was in a video game than a pick-up.

'Too many times. You see, young man, as a marshal one duty was to catch folks who'd jumped bail. You know what that means?' I said that I did, even though I wasn't 100 per cent. 'A lot of them travel to Vegas. Ask me why.'

With the quick fingers of one hand he pulled a pack

of cigarettes from his denim jacket, selected one, found a lighter, lit it and puffed. This was all done in about ten seconds, the cab filling with that sharp smell, despite the Cowboy winding down his window.

'Why?' I asked.

'Because they're fools. They reckon if they can win the jackpot or lay low in a motel long enough we'd forget them. Neither ever happens. They're always caught. Folk can only keep running for so long. It gets tiring.'

'Tell me about it.' (And the Cowboy actually laughed.)

'Why were *you* going to LA with her? What's *your* story?'

I took a deep breath. Did he really want to know? Should I say? I decided to chance telling the truth/welling up.

'I won this all-expenses-paid trip to Hollywood. My poem won a competition—'

'A poem?'

I nodded.

'Well, are you going to share or no?'

'I'd prefer not to.'

The Cowboy shrugged.

'Anyway, I'd have a studio tour, I'd be shown the sights, and I'd be an extra in a superhero movie. But

. . . I missed my connecting flight in Chicago. I should have been there on Tuesday and they were shooting my scene today. At midday.'

'I hate to break it to you, son, but you're not going to make it.'

He took a hand from the steering wheel and pointed a fat finger at the clock in the centre of the dashboard.

Just gone half past eight.

My tiny voice: 'I know.'

'Anyhow, I asked why you were travelling with young Jennifer here. Wouldn't it have been a hell of a lot less hassle if you'd stayed on that Greyhound back there? You'd be in Hollywood by now, doing what you do. Walk of Stars and whatnot. You'd have got there for your filming. Mark my words, she's as crooked as a Virginia fence.'

'What does that mean?'

'Jennifer is stubborn.'

'She tripped over my luggage. That's how she hurt her wrist. I felt kind of responsible. It's okay. I guess your priorities change as you get older.'

'You ain't knee-high to a lamb.'

'No, I mean, like, since meeting Jennifer. I'm older than I was back then.'

There came more chest-rattling laughter. Luckily he didn't start coughing.

'You don't think I never ran away from home when I was a kid, son? I understand.'

Was he smirking? Was that an actual smirk in the corner of his mouth, hiding underneath the plentiful hair of his moustache?

'So how'd you find us? Again? Did you have a tracker? Like Batman?'

As he glanced over, his face softened. He looked as if he could have been someone's grandfather rather than a gnarly old gunslinger.

'Pardon me?'

'Batman uses a tracking device shaped like a bat.'

'I'm sure he does.'

He didn't sound impressed. I'd avoid further superhero chat.

'I'm not a geek. Like, coming to America has kind of put me off all that.'

'Makes no difference to me, son. There's no shame in liking what you like. Hell, I used to collect stamps when I was your age. They probably don't exist any more. No, I used . . . older ways of tracking you. A few tricks I picked up. And, don't be telling anyone

225

this, but you two being dressed up in fancy dress half the time I was running you down kinda made spotting you easier.'

'Jennifer –' I checked she was still asleep before continuing – 'she really thought it was her mum in there. Or, you know, the ashes.' I persevered. 'I think she thought she was doing the right thing, bringing it to LA. You should have seen her face when I broke it. I thought she was going to collapse. And then all the money fell out and . . . what was all that stuff?'

'You want to take some advice from an old timer, son, and not ask too many questions about your friend's grandmother. I'll leave it to your imagination why someone might want to hide away that kind of loot.'

I didn't give up.

'Jennifer was going to see her dad. He's in prison. She wanted to be a family again. Did you know that?'

'Her father?'

'Like I said, she didn't know there was money in the urn. She just wanted to be with her dad.'

'She tell you that?'

'She did. And, I mean, I can deal with missing the movie shoot but it's pretty sad that Jennifer didn't get to see her dad. Family, you know? I mean, I miss mine and they're a nightmare and I've only been away for a couple of days. Seems harsh on her.'

Cigarette between fingers, he dropped open his mouth like he had something to say. But, instead, he raised a hand to scratch the white stubble on his chin. He cleared his throat.

'Nothing more important than your family, Jacob,' he said, his voice quieter now, more like he was talking to himself.

'What's *your* name?' I asked. 'Sir?'

(Americans respond well to being called 'sir'.)

I swear the thick bark of his face reddened. A tiny amount. The smallest blush ever recorded, but still . . .

'Why d'you want to know?'

'It's just . . .' I shrugged. 'You know mine. Seems weird.'

'Dorothy Cave.' I raised a hand to my mouth. 'Go ahead,' he said, even smiling. 'I've heard it all before.'

'Dorothy?'

'Call me Dot if you have to call me anything. My mother, God rest her soul, was crazy about *The Wizard of Oz*. Only had the one child, which was kind of rare back then. Anyhow, when she was pregnant, she and my father decided to call the baby Dorothy. Caused me no

227

end of grief along the way and no denying it. Sometimes I wonder whether I'd have ended up working in an office if they'd called me Michael.'

He flicked his cigarette stub out of the window, winding it up.

We came off the main road and drove down streets of pretty bungalows, stopping for red lights hanging from wires that stretched across the streets. Each house had a perfect front lawn. Trees lined our path. The sudden green gave the place a weird otherness, like an app with the colour settings turned to max.

If this *was* Las Vegas, it wasn't how I imagined it. There wasn't a single miniature Eiffel Tower. There were no neon lights. And I'd seen nobody dressed as Elvis. In fact, I'd seen nobody.

'Jacob,' said the Cowboy. 'Your heart's in the right place. Don't you let nobody tell you otherwise.'

CHAPTER 33

Family Disturbance

We stopped in a motel parking lot. The place was called the Pentagon. I hoped this was down to the building's shape and not because of links to the military. A metal sign erupted from the sidewalk. It was topped by a red square that once said MOTEL but now said MOTE. You could see a ghost imprint of the L if you squinted. Behind it rose a bank of tall buildings, casinos and hotels. They stuck out like broken teeth.

And even though the Cowboy had pulled up the truck with the same abruptness as he might halt a galloping horse, Jennifer sat with her eyes closed, the seat belt having stopped her from smashing her face against the dashboard. Luckily.

He turned to pull the urn bag and its beyond-valuable contents from the space behind our seats.

'We need to freshen up. We need to eat. You wait here while I arrange a room.' He opened the driver's door but paused before getting out. 'You got any money, partner?'

Initially I thought he was asking to borrow some or even have me pay for my share of the motel. But when I shook my head he pulled a wallet from the inside pocket of his coat. It was made from the same snakeskin material as his boots. He took out two fifty-dollar notes (from a wedge of many more) and, stretching across Jennifer, handed them over. I was too confused to accept them straight off, so he waved them in my face.

'Take them,' he said. 'It's important to carry cash, whatever your situation. This is America.' I didn't want to argue, especially as he was staring me down with eyes like black pool balls. He watched me stuff the money into my jeans. 'You say there's a hotel room waiting for you in LA?'

I nodded, reciting the remembered address: 'The Hollywood Roosevelt, 7000 Hollywood Boulevard, Los Angeles.'

He sucked his teeth. It made a strange whining sound.

'I'm a father,' he said, suck done. 'Grandfather too. Can you believe it? One kid in Chicago, the other Kentucky.' He looked to Jennifer. 'Children need to be with their parents. Nothing more important than that. Nothing.' He turned to me. 'I bet your folks are very proud. They've sure brought you up well.' He opened the driver's door. 'Stay out of trouble, Jacob.' The door slammed behind him as he strode off. The noise shuddered across the car park like a firecracker. I watched him pass through the motel's automatic doors and disappear into the shadows.

I looked to the passenger door and, in particular, at the plastic release that would open it if pulled. Jennifer's eyes remained closed.

THE COWBOY WAS LETTING US GO!

The realisation flashed like the lights of a Vegas casino.

Trembling fingers pulled at the handle. The door, creaking, opened.

'Jennifer, Jennifer,' I said. 'You won't believe it.'

I shook her. Waking, her face looked anything but relaxed.

'What?' she said. 'What are you doing? Stop shaking me.'

'We've stopped, he's gone, the doors are unlocked.'

She blinked herself fully awake, turning her head to look through the pick-up's side window.

'See!' I said, stepping out of the cab, thinking Jennifer would follow. But she didn't even release her seat belt. She just sat there. Blinking and yawning, yawning and blinking.

'No,' she said, as I stood slack-jawed at the passenger side. 'I blew up an RV, remember. Like, totally exploded it.'

The motel's entrance stayed quiet but this wouldn't last. Soon the Cowboy would come moseying out.

'But he wants us to go,' I said. 'That's why he left. I've been talking to him. He's not all bad. He's, like, chill. He's got kids.'

Jennifer reverted to her earlier position – eyes closed, back straight, facing forward. I knew I needed to be extra special, superhero persuasive now. I thought back to English lessons. There was one a couple of years ago where the teacher made us write to Father Christmas, asking for presents, but using *persuasive techniques*.

Could I remember any of them? Rhetorical questions? Humour? List of three?

The sun flashed off the motel's automatic doors. A

man stepped out. He wasn't wearing a cowboy hat; he wore a UPS baseball cap.

'We've got this far, Jennifer. You and me. All the way from Chicago. How many miles is that?'

'Thousands.'

'Thousands, right. *And* you're only fourteen. You know, I'd thought you were seventeen or something. Not that it makes any difference. I was talking to the Cowboy and he told me his name's Dorothy.' Her face was unmoving. 'Look, if you're going to get shipped back to your grandmother either way, we may as well make the last day fun, right? When I won the competition to be in the superhero film, I was more excited than I'd ever been. I couldn't think of anything I'd rather do. And then I met you and, you know, it sucks that I missed the shoot, super sucks, and I thought I'd feel worse but . . . I don't!'

There! She smiled! And I even almost meant what I was saying! Her eyes were still closed, though.

'And it'd be nice to see your dad, right? We could get a burger too.'

Her eyes flashed open and I think if she'd laughed or turned me down, I would have shrunk into a tiny shrivelled doll and would have continued shrinking until, *pop,* I blinked into nothing.

But she didn't. Instead she said, 'You're so corny, and always with the food. And, for real, his name is Dorothy?'

I nodded.

'Ha!' she said. 'I almost feel sorry for him.'

I did the 'so' thing with my hands and turned my smile upside down.

'Okay, okay. I was kidding. Sure, I'm coming. I was always coming. I was enjoying your speech, that's all. And it sounded important for your continuing development.'

I hated/loved her.

Leaving, I turned to see a figure standing at the motel entrance. The sun glared from the glass of the doors. The bright reflection made it difficult to see clearly. But I'm sure the man wore a cowboy hat. And from under a cloud of cigarette smoke I'm sure too that he raised a hand in farewell.

CHAPTER 34

The Strip

We jumped on a bus. And the thing about the Strip was that I'd seen it all before a thousand times in the films and TV shows set here.

There was the miniature Statue of Liberty, although the Vegas version still towered over the huge Stars and Stripes fluttering from a flagpole at its base. Behind was a huddle of fake old buildings. Rising over these was the red spaghetti track of a roller coaster. The Strip must have been designed by a kid who'd drunk too many sugary drinks and knew America only through Google Image searches.

That was the only possible explanation.

Look! The MGM Grand, with a monstrous metal lion on a pedestal the size of a football pitch. The thick green sign advertising the casino threw a shadow over the road like a giant's tombstone. There was a Hershey's building, done up to look like a chocolate bar (another stomach rumble as we passed). And check out the food hall with its accompanying Coca-Cola bottle made from real glass and bigger than my house. Alongside it were three M&M characters, their wrinkled lips frozen for eternity. They were bigger than our bus. It'd be terrifying if they came alive.

Jennifer leant across the aisle. 'Is there an Amtrak station nearby?' she asked a woman.

The stranger grinned back. 'No. Sorry, babe. There ain't no trains coming through Vegas and there's not been for as long as I've lived here! We're like one of the largest cities in the whole of the States to be without a rail service. Google it.' And she continued smiling as if she were, like, proud of this. She'll have noticed the exact opposite expression on our two faces. 'I'll tell you what there is, though!'

'What?' asked Jennifer.

'A Greyhound depot! And ain't that just as good?'

Jennifer bought two tickets from a teenager in a baseball cap who spent more time looking at his phone (*so* lucky) than he did her. This bus station had been built to serve trains. It had the high ceilings and shiny floor tiles you'd expect. We found a space and we sat and we waited as the hour opened up before us like a physics test.

'Why are there no trains in Las Vegas?' I asked.

'Because America,' she replied, adding, 'Times like this I miss my phone.'

We sat shoulder to shoulder, reading the subtitles of a muted news report on a huge TV suspended in the corner of this, the waiting room.

Jennifer's comment had got me thinking. I couldn't put it off any longer. I had to call home.

'Can I borrow the credit card?' I asked. Jennifer nodded. 'I think I'm going to ring my parents.'

She kind of grunted and passed me the card. I stood and hiked up my jeans like I was about to take part in a gunfight on Main Street. (And feeling like I'd never worn any other boxer shorts than these.)

'Well . . . it's time to receive the biggest bollocking of my whole life.'

'Bollocking?' said Jennifer.

'You know. Like getting shouted at.'

'Okay. Who cares? I blew up an RV and stole my grandmother's fortune.'

(*She has a point*, I thought.)

In between the lockers and the toilets were three

phones. I picked up a black handset and pushed the card into the machine. I looked over to Jennifer sitting in the bank of seats across the way. She put a thumb up. I turned back, a dull headache forming, and dialled the number. The phone must have rung at most two times before someone answered.

'Yeah?'

It was my sister again. The worst of the three possibilities.

'Hi,' I said. 'Let me speak to one of them.'

Amy laughed. I've got to admit – this reaction, it broke my thinking. She's only ever happy when bad stuff's about to happen.

'Muuum! Daaaad! He's alive!!!' I could hear her shouting.

There was a mouselike rustling on the line as I felt the whirlpool in my stomach that always comes when I'm in big trouble because, really, what *had* I been thinking? Now, at this Vegas payphone, it felt as if I'd finally woken from a strange dream and, yes, Jennifer, I did care about bollockings.

'Jacob?' It was Mum. That was one thing. 'Where are you? Amy said something about being on a plane in Albuquerque. I've been worrying myself sick. Tell us you're in LA at least. We're on speakerphone.'

My soul sank at the 's' word.

'First of all: everything is going well. Really well. And there's absolutely nothing to worry about.'

(I need to improve my acting if I want to make an impact in Hollywood.)

'Are you in Los Angeles?' demanded Dad.

'Not quite. Almost. But . . . I ended up getting a lift.'

'A lift? With who? Where are you? Can you hear how unhappy I am?'

'I'm in Las Vegas.'

'Las Vegas! What are you doing there? Las Vegas! Have you been kidnapped? Should I ring the police? You don't have to say anything incriminating, just yes or no,' said Mum. 'Is it the Mafia?'

'He's not been kidnapped. He's an idiot,' said Dad.

'No, Mum. Dad—'

'No, you've not been kidnapped or—'

'I've not been kidnapped.' And I found (a tiny amount of) confidence from the realisation that, actually, I hadn't been kidnapped, not really, and I *had* got all this way. And, yes, I could do with a shower and I'd love to brush my teeth, but, like Amy said, I *wasn't* dead, which was good. 'I'm going to be in LA by the end of the day. I'm just a little behind schedule, that's all.'

'Jacob?' asked Dad in a concrete voice. 'What do you think you're doing?'

I held the phone away from my ear to reduce the impact of his voice.

'Improvising,' I said. 'Being proactive.'

'Impro-what?'

'Like you—'

He cut me off.

'End of the day? You miss that film and you're grounded for eternity. No PlayStation, no nothing. Your social life will be finished. Do you understand?'

(In different circumstances I might have asked, 'What social life?')

'Yes,' I said. 'Sorry. Umm . . .'

Didn't he *know* I'd missed it? Didn't he *know* the scene was due to be shot pretty much now? Time to be brave and admit everything. Because there was only so much they could do when they were thousands of miles away.

'Yeaaaah,' I said. 'Sooooo.'

There was a pause. I could hear Dad lick his lips. Mum's voice droned unintelligibly in the background.

'What happened to your phone? Were you mugged?' I made a noise like 'agh' that was prevented from turning into a word by Dad continuing. 'You go straight to that studio or the hotel or whatever and you make sure you turn up on time, you hear me? I've told half of Somerset about you being in this bloody film.'

'About that . . . I just wanted to say I'm safe.'

(*And* a massive coward.)

Mum spoke – the sugar to make the poison palatable.

'Look, the reason we're all worked up is that the studio called.'

They knew! They knew I'd missed the scene! That's why Amy had sounded so happy! It had been a good life, kind of . . . I wish I'd eaten more adventurously. It might have been interesting to have had a girlfriend. The kissing. The hand-holding. People go mad for all that.

But . . . wait . . . hadn't Dad threatened me with an eternal grounding *if* I missed the shoot? Something wasn't right.

Mum continued: 'Your scene, the one you're supposed to be in the background for?'

'Yeah?'

'They changed plans because of the snow. You weren't the only one stuck in Chicago. They're half a day behind schedule, Jacob.'

'For God's sake, they're shooting tonight!' shouted Dad. 'Didn't you know?'

My brain turned into a question mark. How *could* I have known?

'Yes, definitely tonight, I think,' said Mum. 'Your tonight. It's so confusing with the time difference. Wait a mo. I've written it down somewhere.' I couldn't hear the mutterings. 'You're eight hours behind, right?'

'Mum?' I said. 'What did they say?'

'Yes, plans have changed – they're shooting tonight! You've got enough time.'

Goodbyes were said, promises were made. Back in the waiting area, Jennifer asked if I was still alive.

(People seemed to really care about my mortality.)

'Get this,' I said, trying not to smile from ear to ear as my heart beat with birthday excitement. 'They've not shot my scene. If I get there today, there's still a chance I'll be in the superhero movie. Fortune and glory. Hollywood and all that. It takes, like, four hours, right? There's still hope, Jennifer.' I remembered that I was a teenage boy talking to a teenage girl. 'But, you know, if I miss it, I miss it and that's cool too. Whatever.'

'Great news,' said Jennifer. 'Really great news. The hope.' Her face told a different story. 'The bus takes five hours, by the way.'

Nothing Happened
California

And for the first time in America nothing happened. Mostly because Jennifer wasn't talking, like she'd suddenly turned shy or tired. She made me take the aisle seat. I didn't argue. There were people around and I was becoming hyper-aware of my accent.

She sat with the sweatshirt collar caught on her chin. Her sleeve was pulled over the fingers of her good hand. And like that she remained, eyes closed, half tortoise, until we were well into the desert. Every so often I looked at her out of the corner of my eye and tried not to feel guilty because, really, I had nothing to feel guilty about.

'You okay?' I asked at one point.

'Yeah,' she said. 'We're almost there, aren't we? Almost finished.'

'Almost' meant about five and a half hours to get to LA. There was no book this time. Unlike Homer, it was a peaceful journey. The only act of violence happened when I went to the toilet. My stomach wasn't used to the 'all-American' breakfast burrito I'd had back at the bus station.

When I returned to my seat, Jennifer was asleep or, at least, pretending to be. And the Greyhound continued through the bright desert, a silver bullet following a black shadow. I tried visualising what waited in Hollywood. I'd not worry about anything else. If I missed the scene, I'd enjoy the hotel. I could even ask Jennifer if she wanted to stay over.

No, she'd think me weird.

Imagine staying in a hotel. Imagine standing in a hot shower. Imagine a complimentary toothbrush. Imagine pillows. Proper plump. Imagine cushions. Fluffy too. Imagine saying goodbye to Jennifer.

I needed to take control of my thoughts. They ranged like an untrained dog.

The director would shake my hand. He'd introduce me to the star. We'd chat about Britain and he'd compliment my clothes and . . . *Would I be wearing the Navajo top with its grease stains from breakfast? It smells*

like Jennifer. Maybe I should ask if she wants to come to the studio? Would they let me do that? She could watch? How awkward? What about her dad? Was he really in prison? That's why she's upset. I'd not asked. What's wrong with me? I should lock myself in my bedroom and never come out. If I ever get back to Somerset.

A face hovering over the seat ahead broke my thinking. It was a kid with a baseball cap and braces. Chubby fingers gripped the head cushion. His mother, or at least the woman he was travelling with, snored in the chair alongside. The noise she made was the same pitch as the engine's whine. It was weird.

'Are you Scottish?' asked the face.

'No,' I said. 'Sorry.'

The face disappeared. As I readied myself for more visualisation, the face popped up again.

'Are you sure?' it asked. 'I heard you arguing with your girlfriend.'

'I'm pretty sure. I'm from Britain, though, and Scotland's part of it.'

At this information the boy's cheeks trembled with delight.

'Wait there!' he said and vanished. When he returned, he had an iPad in his hands, balanced on the chair head. 'Can I ask you some questions? It's for an assignment.'

I nodded because there was nothing else to do right now apart from the whole feeling uncertain about the future thing.

'One. Have you ever met the queen?'

'No.'

With his tongue between his teeth the boy made a note of my answer with a longer-than-expected series of finger strokes.

'Two. Have you ever assaulted someone at a soccer match?'

'No,' I replied.

Again his fingers entered my response.

'And finally, number three, do you regularly see the dentist?'

'What kind of assignment is this?' I asked.

'National stereotypes,' came the response and I explained that Mum made me visit the dentist every six months.

'Thank you for your responses. They have been successfully recorded.'

'Is your iPad on the internet? Can I borrow it for, like, one second? I need to work out how to get to Hollywood.'

'No,' said the boy. 'But you can borrow Mom's.'

I did just that, agreeing that I'd have to pretend to have stolen it if she woke, which she wouldn't do because she'd taken one of her pills, you know how it is.

Opening Google Maps, I already understood that Twin Towers Correctional Facility (I'd remembered the name because you couldn't forget it) wouldn't be anywhere near the Hollywood Roosevelt because nothing's ever easy when you're me and/or away from home.

The jail was half an hour's walk from the bus station. And, yes, Hollywood was so far distant, I had to use a two-finger zoom to get both places on the same screen. I guess you can't have all those celebrity types mingling with criminals.

Later, after handing the tablet back to the kid, and seeing Jennifer's eyes were open, I wondered out loud whether she might like to come to Hollywood with me. If she was upset because I'd not already asked, it was because I thought she'd just come if she wanted to and it really wasn't a big deal and was it me or was it, like, really hot in this bus?

'I'm not angry,' she smiled. 'It's the fact that the time with my dad will be severely limited because I'm liable to be hauled back to Chicago by the police, not to mention

I ran off in the first place because I thought I was reuniting the family, which, obviously, I'm not. And, like, I've got no idea where my mom's ashes actually are and that's a downer. All that *and* end-of-vacation blues. But I'm fine.'

The tiny cogs in my brain turned.

'I mean, you could come to Hollywood first and *then* see your dad? It's not like he's going anywhere.'

I thought this was funny but she wasn't laughing. Instead there came a long sigh, followed by a long string of words.

'The police, Jacob. They'll be waiting. And even if they're not, Dad'll make me do the right thing because . . . dads. You know what they're like. Right? It's voodoo.'

Everyone likes to think that when it's their turn to step onstage for the important speech, the moment that brings the whole story together, they'll know what to say. Mainly because their lines have been written for them. But life doesn't really work like that.

'True,' I said.

Jennifer reached out for my hand. She squeezed it. Almost enough to hurt. Almost. The contact pushed idiot words out of my mouth.

'I don't even know when the shoot is taking place other than sometime tonight, so . . .'

She pulled back as the gopher head of the baseball cap and braces kid appeared again. He addressed Jennifer.

'Hey,' he said. 'Would you answer some questions for an assignment?'

'Stick your questions up your butt,' she replied.

The boy dropped out of view. Jennifer and I reflected smiles back at each other. I held up a palm for a high-five but she left me hanging.

CHAPTER 36

The Princess Returns
Los Angeles, California

I arrived in LA. Around two days later than originally planned.

'Evening starts at six, right?' I asked Jennifer as we got off the bus. 'It's the same here as Britain?'

She didn't answer but I knew I was running out of time. It was like playing a video game and being saved from GAME OVER by winning an extra life, only to lose it a second later by falling into a pit of spikes.

Still, they call it the City of Angels because it's where miracles happen.

We said to the Greyhound guy behind a computer that we'd accidentally left our baggage on an earlier bus and was there any chance he had it? We filled out a form with one of those pens chained to its holder.

'I'll look,' he said when we were done.

He disappeared through a door behind his desk and came back with the Princess and the rest of our stuff.

I'd never seen Jennifer look so surprised. She was kind of more shocked than anything. The first thing we did was to check our phones. Both were out of battery. The second thing was to put on our coats. They smelt weird – I think because they were clean.

Pulling the Princess behind me, we left the bus station to be reborn into the Californian afternoon. If our possessions had been returned so easily, maybe everything *would* work out okay in the end? Like with me being a famous actor, for instance?

'Anyway, are you on Facebook?'

I knew I sounded like someone's awkward uncle. I didn't care.

Jennifer blinked, confused, like a GIF.

'One: what's that got to do with anything? And, two, who uses Facebook?'

I persevered. Sometimes you've got to take the risk that you're going to look stupid. I let go of the Princess and she clattered over behind me, like the bag was causing a scene, desperate for attention.

'I've not really been using it since my parents got an

account, but there's Instagram or WhatsApp, like, if we wanted to keep in contact? Snapchat? We wouldn't have to worry about streaks or anything. I'm just saying.'

'You don't have to list all the social media apps,' she said, but smiling.

I tried to think of others because that might be funny.

'Umm . . .' But I couldn't and this made things more awkward than they should have been. 'I mean, I *could* give you my number? Is there an international code? You've got a phone? I've seen your phone. Okay. But you know—'

Her features jumped – a sudden thought.

'I owe you something!' she said and, looking left and right, grabbed my arm to lead me and the Princess away from the bus station. 'Before we split up. I almost forgot.'

The neighbourhood looked like it was between jobs. Opposite was a row of shopfronts, but only two were open. Of these, one was a 'punk store' with a BMX propped up outside, the wheels tied together with a heavy-looking chain. The other, a few spaces down, had a sign above its dirty canopy, reading VICKY'S 99-CENT STORE. The other shopfronts had metallic grilles rolled down. Tags had been sprayed on everything like an overeager mother with your uniforms the day before a new school year.

But where was Jennifer taking me? And what would she give me? Obviously a kiss goodbye would be inappropriate. Maybe she had her number on a piece of paper and wanted to hand it over? Why she'd want to do this in secret, I didn't know, but Jennifer *was* puzzling. That was (partly) why I liked her.

We stopped on a side street that cut between the fenced-off Greyhound lot, its huge sign casting a shadow over us, and a 'city center' car park (empty). And as I looked up at the corporate logo of a running dog, I thought I could do without travelling on another one of their buses. For a few years at least.

'Why are you staring at the sky?' asked Jennifer. 'The action's down here. Take this.'

And I felt weirdly disappointed when she pulled out cash.

'Two hundred,' she said, thumbing the money out like people do with American banknotes. 'I took it from the stash. It's only fair and Dad will pay it back. My grandmother won't even notice. Just to see you safely to Hollywood. Because I owe you.'

Why were people suddenly desperate to give me

money? I was about to do the decent thing and refuse it or, at least, only take enough to not seem rude . . .

But then . . .

There was a sharp pain in my side. Jennifer gasped and a strange hand, smelling of coffee, clamped over my mouth. I saw light flashing off a blade.

'Give me the cash. All the cash. Give me your phones too. Any jewellery? Give me that. I'm mad as hell – don't mess with me, kids.'

He took his hand from me and I spun away, a frantic ballerina. I bounced into Jennifer. We now both faced the mugger, our three figures frozen like a drama lesson tableau called 'inner-city crime'.

The knifeman wore a suit and tie but maybe that was an American thing. Approaching us, he took a step over the Princess, who lay on her side, terrified.

'Come on, kids, I'm not joking here.'

He looked frantically left and right. His free hand waved beckoning fingers. Jennifer still gripped the dollars in her hand. Her eyes flicked from the man down to the Princess and moved to me. I nodded, understanding.

We each pushed a flat palm against the man's chest. The two of us created sufficient force to bump him backwards, his heels meeting the pink skin of the Princess, his body flying backwards and crashing down on to the sidewalk.

'Rescue the Princess,' hissed Jennifer and I did. 'Run!' she yelled, and I did.

We raced back on to the main road, the suitcase's wheels bouncing behind us. When we judged we were far enough away, we slowed down. Despite all the recent exercise, I was panting and could feel an embarrassing armpit wetness.

'If anyone's a superhero,' smiled Jennifer, 'it's the suitcase. Did you see her take out that dude?'

I nodded, returning the smile.

'I never used to be a fan.' I patted the Princess. 'But that's changed. Maybe I'll buy her a cape or something. By the way, I can send you back the cash when . . .'

My voice faded. We smiled. A car passed. The Princess, as modest as ever, sat there saying nothing.

'I guess this is it, then,' said Jennifer with a shrug. 'I'll watch out for you in the theatre. Not that I ever go. It's been fun.'

'What theatre?'

'For your movie.'

My stomach churned and, this time, it wasn't because of the Vegas breakfast.

'Right,' I said. 'So you *actually* don't want to come with me?'

'I've got to see Dad, Jacob. Before they catch me again and I'm sent back. We've been through this.' I narrowed my eyes as I studied her. 'But you've got to go. Don't stop believing and all. Your big chance.' A pause. 'You can't miss your movie, Jacob.'

But she made it sound like a question. Like she was asking if I *really* had to leave her. Right now, she looked younger than fourteen.

Silence filled the space like a giant wedge. She held out her good arm in a hug invitation. I didn't need further encouragement to dive in.

We stood on a downtown corner, in LA, cuddling. She was warm and smelt of travelling. A car sounded its horn. The driver shouted, 'You go, bruh!'

I pulled back.

'Your dad's –' I hesitated, trying to think of a better word than 'prison' – 'place is straight up a road called S Alameda Street. I borrowed this kid's iPad on the coach. It's, like, half an hour's walk.'

'Thanks,' said Jennifer. 'Appreciated. "S" is for south FYI.'

'My email address is jacobbowserjacob@gmail.com. I

used to be into Mario. Like, really into Mario. But it's easy to remember, so . . .'

She laughed. I decided that I liked the sound.

'Thanks, Luigi,' she said. 'I won't forget it. There are worse things to be into. Like superheroes, kidding, kidding. And I think we made a pretty good team. You and me. So . . . just . . . good luck with your movie. Don't forget me when you're famous.'

And she turned. And she walked away. Because, and Jennifer will tell you this too, there aren't always happy endings. Because there's always going to be that scene when you're left on your own.

And I'm sure she *was* kidding about the superhero comment.

'Honestly, I'm still sorry about your wrist,' I called, but my words bounced against her back, lost to LA.

I pulled up the Princess and got going. And it felt like her wheels turned in the wrong direction.

CHAPTER 37

Open Doors

The 720 bus left from E 7th Street. Google had said it'd take twenty minutes to get to Wilshire/Vermont station. I could take the Metro straight to Hollywood from there. The total journey should be just under an hour. That meant I'd arrive in Tinseltown at around six. I'd head straight for the hotel because it was four stars and would have helpful, not scary, people at the front desk who'd tell me what to do.

The bus stop was a flagpole sticking out of the sidewalk. But instead of a flag, it held a modest metal rectangle with the letter M in a circle, the word 'Metro' and three bus numbers, one of which was mine.

I leant against the fence of a smart, but shady, building. The Princess waited at my feet. I had no idea what time the bus might come and there was nobody to ask. Even if there'd been other people waiting, I don't think I'd have had the confidence to speak to them without Jennifer. Like, have you ever met a friendly stranger?

Further worries: was the mugger in the suit nearby? Would he try again if he saw me? Maybe there were other muggers?

I didn't think I looked like someone with money or expensive stuff. My hair was thick with days of unwashing. And I think the stained coat/sweatshirt combo, made me look . . . well . . . not exactly rolling in cash.

She wouldn't be far now. If I jogged, I could still catch her. I'd done a lot of jogging recently. Like someone's dad after his phone had shown his chins through the front-facing camera.

Would Jennifer smile if I tapped her on the shoulder?

'Hollywood can wait,' I'd say, full Cheddar. 'I want to meet your dad. It's not over until then. We're a team, goddamnit.'

And I was struck by that weird thought again: maybe there *was* more to life than getting excited about being an extra in an unnamed superhero film? It might have been filmed already anyway. Imagine how disappointed I'd feel if I left Jennifer for the film, then got there and found I'd missed it all? I could always tell Dad that they cut my scene from the final edit. I didn't *have* to confess.

Now, if I knew for sure it was Spider-Man, that'd be a different story. But they'd have said if it were a marquee hero. The whole secrecy thing was to disguise the disappointment.

Doctor Bong.

An orange bus rolled up. The automatic doors hissed open. The driver turned to me. I could see myself reflected in her sunglasses. My head shook, I mouthed 'sorry', and both of these things took me by surprise because I really hadn't decided anything yet.

A passenger shouted something as the bus drove away. I saw his lips moving but couldn't hear the words. He didn't look happy.

But I didn't care.

Instead I ran, the Princess bouncing behind me over pavement cracks. I was a missile, launched at Jennifer. When I struck her, there wouldn't be death and destruction. There'd be hugs and smiles. Or a raised eyebrow and some sass.

Somerset had never felt so distant.

Foot after foot and it was another one of those roads that went on forever or, at least, to the cloudless sky.

Every so often there were trees probably planted to create a sense of prettiness absent from the whitewashed walls. There were also huge piles of trash, like the rubbish truck had given up this route but residents continued to pile up black bags in the hope that if only they believed someday their refuse services would return, they would.

In short, it wasn't a road to fill you with hope. But I'd made my decision and I kept at it. My forehead was moist with breaking sweat and my insides hurt, especially where the failed mugger had pricked me, but it didn't matter.

Because! There! Boom!

Jennifer was leaning against a telegraph pole outside a brick building, painted yellow, that advertised VINTAGE AND DESIGNER FURNISHINGS. She had her back to me.

I didn't stretch out a hand to touch her shoulder. I thought that might be creepy. Instead I cleared my throat.

'Yo,' I said.

But the word came out exactly when this huge truck passed and it was lost to the rush of the diesel engine.

So I said it again. And this time she turned.

'Finally,' she said. 'What took you so long? You look like a puppy.' She held an ice cream. The corners of her mouth were stained white. 'I mean, it's good to see you. And . . . I like puppies, so . . .'

I spoke quickly, panting. 'I was thinking we could see your dad together, although I wouldn't have to actually go into the . . . place. And then Hollywood afterwards because it's probably on the way and I could even get a taxi maybe because you gave me all that money and . . .'

For a second her chill-whatever-chill mask slipped.

'Thanks for coming back,' she said, beaming, because, you know what, she couldn't help herself. 'I mean, I would have done the same. We're Mario and Luigi. To be honest, I can't believe you left me first time round. Ice-cold.'

'I wanted to stay. You told me to go. It was an order. You ordered me.'

'Why would I ever do that?' she said. 'You're my sidekick, bro.'

We walked together again, our shoulders pretty much touching. And I wanted to say that we were more like Mario and the Princess but sometimes it's better to keep your mouth shut.

CHAPTER 38

Prison Break

'It doesn't look much like a prison,' I said. 'There are no bars.'

We sat on a bench on a corner of grass between thick walls of glass and stone. Two flags fluttered as the space opened up to the road – the Stars and Stripes and the Californian Bear. There was a blue postbox. It was squat and had four legs and might have been an out-of-work *Star Wars* droid.

'What d'you think it looks like?'

'A hotel? But without windows.'

Jennifer gave me such a withering look, I felt my privates shrink.

'So what's the plan? Are we going to have to break

in? Is that it? Will I need to borrow the uniform of a canteen worker and slip past the guards that way?'

'I guess,' she said. 'Or we could ask at reception?'

We didn't have to do either. At that moment Jennifer's dad came running out of the front doors, headed straight for us. He wasn't wearing shackles and there was no pack of police dogs chasing him. Instead he had on a smart brown suit. His round glasses made him look like a professor. He *wasn't* wearing a tie, which might have been either a prison or a casual thing.

'Jennifer!' he said, half in exasperation, half in excitement. If you can imagine that. 'I saw you from my office. What are you doing? What have you done this time?'

Jennifer was already up and one-arm cuddling him. And I felt like I needed to stand too because Jennifer and her dad were and to stay sitting would be awkward. Jennifer's dad pushed her back from the embrace, his hands on her shoulders.

'And what's up with your arm?' he said. 'Are you hurt?'

Jennifer gave a 'it's a long story' roll of the eyes.

'It's more of a fashion thing. My arm's fine.'

Her dad didn't even blink.

'Jenny, Jenny, Jenny. Ah, it's good to see you. But why are you here, honey? What's going on?' He didn't wait for answers. He could read his daughter's face. 'Come on, Jennifer. You know what this means. You know the trouble . . . How'd you get here? I can't . . .'

It was at this point that he acknowledged me, Mr Awks, standing there, staring at my shoes. He held out a hand, which I shook. It was an adult gesture but it had the effect of making me feel eight years old.

'This is Jacob,' said Jennifer, her voice weirdly constricted, quiet. 'I got here because of him. Kind of. And he's British, so you might struggle to understand him at first. Over time, it gets easier, though. Like riding a bike. He's my friend.'

'So you're to blame?' asked Dad, waving a fist in my face but in a pretend way, I was hoping.

'I'm fourteen,' I said but I'm not sure why.

'You know, Jacob, she's normally such a quiet girl. I don't think she's ever left Illinois before. Have you left Illinois?' Her mouth dropped open. 'You won't believe how many times her grandmother has called.' He turned to Jennifer. 'You won't believe how many times your grandmother has called. She's worried about you, girl.'

Jennifer grunted. 'I doubt it.'

'Jenny. I love you, you know I do, but what's happening here?'

Jennifer spoke like a shower. Words came raining down on her dad. About how she wasn't running away from home, about how she'd taken her mum's ashes, about what was really inside the urn, about reuniting the family now that Dad was back.

When she was finished, Mr Lewis looked from me to Jennifer, shaking his head. The way his mouth was slanted, though, almost in a grin, suggested he wasn't too angry. He almost looked impressed.

'Girl,' he said. 'My little girl. Look, there's a Denny's a block away. Let's go and talk strategy, grab some food. Wait here while I finish off inside, yeah? On the way you can explain the whole sling as a fashion-statement thing.'

It turned out that he wasn't a prisoner. He was a counsellor, which meant, I guess, talking to prisoners about how they felt to be locked up. I wouldn't guess they'd feel too pleased, especially if they had to keep describing these feelings, but I was no counsellor. It was his first job outside the army, the first time he'd actually lived somewhere.

Me, I never admitted that I'd assumed he was a criminal, hoping that Jennifer thought all that earlier chat about breaking him out was only more evidence of my British sense of humour.

(Jennifer didn't mention my Hollywood appointment and I didn't want to buzzkill the reunion between father and daughter. Serious stuff was happening. You could tell by the way Jennifer had gone all quiet.)

Denny's was like McDonald's but an American diner with plates. The place was dotted with faces chowing down on heart-troubling food. The waitress greeted Jennifer's dad by name (Mr Lewis).

'Do *your* parents know you're here?' asked Mr Lewis as we slid into a booth – me and Jennifer facing him. 'How did you two . . . get together? For want of a better phrase.'

'Kind of,' I said. 'They kind of know I'm here.'

'Jacob's got a great story,' said Jennifer at the same time. 'Tell him, Jacob.'

The waitress appeared and flopped four A3 laminated menus down. She asked if we wanted drinks. Mr Lewis opted for a coffee and Jennifer asked for two Cokes without checking with me, which was fine.

I'll just have something to eat and then I'll get going. It'd be rude to get up and leave right now. I've only just met the man. Thirty minutes won't make any difference, despite what the marching ants in my stomach are saying.

'Superheroes,' I said.

Mr Lewis looked confused.

'Marvel,' she spoke to me, despite fixing her dad with a toothy grin. 'The competition. The hotel. Tell him.'

'I'm more interested in the whole "Do Jacob's parents know what he's doing and where he is" thing,' said Mr Lewis. 'Do you live in LA, Jacob?'

'So I won a competition to appear in a Marvel film as an extra. I wrote a poem. But, you know . . .'

'Which character? Batman?' asked Mr Lewis, sounding as if he were genuinely impressed.

Jennifer smiled and covered her mouth with a quick hand.

'It's top secret. They wouldn't say. Jennifer thinks it's She-Hulk but I don't even care. And Batman's DC, so—'

'And the studio paid for his flights from England and, like, this five-star Hollywood hotel and spending money and all these touristy things,' said Jennifer.

Mr Lewis sipped from his coffee, nodding.

'So how was it?' he said, mid-sip.

I turned to Jennifer. 'I was meant to arrive on Tuesday but . . . haven't got there yet.'

And Mr Lewis did something I've only ever seen on TV: he sprayed coffee from his mouth in shock. Jennifer was quick with the napkins, pulled from our table's silver dispenser. Mr Lewis was almost as fast with his apology.

'They're shooting tonight,' said Jennifer. 'He's spent the week helping me get here. It's a long story. And journey. There was an accident in Chicago.'

'And snow,' I said.

'Why aren't you there, like, now?' said Mr Lewis, pulling a napkin across the table. Having mopped up the coffee, he checked his phone. 'What time tonight? It's pretty much six already, Jacob. You know most of the studios are out of town?' Wait. Are you two messing with me?' We shook our heads like wet dogs drying. Mr Lewis wagged a finger. 'Are you crazy, kid? You don't get repeat shots at Hollywood. You're speaking to an expert here. The prison's full of missed chances.'

I shook my head. Even though I wasn't entirely sure that I wasn't crazy. Because why hadn't I gone straight to Hollywood? I mean, I *could* have met up with Jennifer afterwards. For all her talk of the police we'd managed to get here without being arrested. Maybe it was my hormones again? I'd do a Google when my phone was charged next.

Already Mr Lewis was up and out of the booth, pulling out a handful of bills to pay for the drinks.

'We're getting you to Hollywood. You can chill with Jennifer later. Hell. No friend of Jenny's is turning down the chance of starring in a superhero picture.'

'I'm only an extra,' I said, but he was already stepping away, car keys in hand.

'Dad's a man of action,' said Jennifer, as we squeaked from the booth's fake leather. 'I so wish I took after him.'

CHAPTER 39

Freeways in Los Angeles

'My name is Jacob Clark. I won a competition to be in a film. And I was supposed to get here on Tuesday but was delayed. Sorry about that. Thanks.'

I sat in a back seat of Mr Lewis's Toyota. Jennifer had insisted she sit in the passenger seat. The car wasn't moving. Ahead were infinite brake lights. All around us were stationary cars. We were part of a solid whole, a metal snake suffocating Los Angeles.

Rush hour. American style.

'Please hold, Mr Clark, while I connect you.'

'Pretend to be someone who's assertive,' said Jennifer.

I'd used Mr Lewis's phone to get on my Gmail. Along with all the marketing messages from Somerset's premier pizza restaurants and four emails from Mum, of increasing panic and desperation, there was an email from the studio.

Basically it said that they understood there'd been difficulties with transportation from Chicago and I wasn't the only one affected but, importantly, it also gave me a phone number to ring when finally in LA.

'Jacob!' It was a woman's voice and if Hollywood possessed a particular accent, it was this. 'First off, have you spoken to your parents? You've spoken to your parents, right?'

'Yep,' I said.

'Great. You had us all anxious there. We don't want a Netflix doc about the prize-winning kid who went missing.'

'I took a Greyhound.'

'Did you go via Hawaii? I'm kidding. I'm kidding.'

'There were . . . some problems.'

At this Jennifer swung round from the front. She offered the largest smile I'd ever seen. It stretched from ear to ear. My eyes flicked to the rear-view mirror. And although I could only see Mr Lewis's eyes and eyebrows, I could tell he really *wasn't* smiling.

'Where are you now, Jacob? I'm hoping you're going to say pretty close. Like two blocks away close. You heard we're running your scene tonight, right?'

'Yeah. My dad said.'

'Here's the thing. We're shooting in an hour. Which means you need to be at the lot in, like, a bare minimum of thirty minutes for costume and make-up and paperwork. Where are you right now? Are you going to make it?'

I lifted the phone from my ear and put my hand over the microphone.

'Where are we?' I asked.

'Los Angeles,' said Jennifer, still grinning. 'That's in California.'

I ignored her. She could be annoying sometimes.

'Coming out of Little Tokyo,' said Mr Lewis.

'How far's that from Hollywood?'

'Should be fifteen minutes,' he replied. He opened his hands from the steering wheel to indicate the solid traffic. 'But now? Who knows, kid. LA traffic.'

I reported back to the studio woman.

'I'm afraid to say, Jacob, with the schedule already delayed I don't think they'll be open to waiting on your behalf. Time is money, you know. Obviously it goes without saying that the rest of the prize, or what's left, remains valid. I'm sure we can arrange merch and a tour and you've got your spending allowance still.' She heard the silence coming from my end. 'Autographs, even? Maybe a meet and greet?'

'But if I get there in half an hour, I can still make it?'

'Sure thing, honey.'

I licked my lips, daring to ask the question.

'Are you allowed to say what you're filming? I know it's top secret. But . . .'

'It's the new Spider-Man project, Jacob. Are you a fan?'

A star exploded in my mind. A whole galaxy destroyed. The universe.

'No way. For real?'

'Uh-huh.'

Like I'd fallen into a deep freezer, I felt my everything stiffen. Maybe not everything. Mainly my resolve. I'd seen enough films and played enough video games to realise there were ways round gridlock in American cities. I might not have ropes made from super-strong spiderweb, but I had a car. Driven by a prison counsellor.

And that should sound more impressive.

'I'll be there,' I said. 'Tell the director. No problemo.'

(I don't know why I used that last word.)

'Okay, Jacob, it's just gone six now. We'll be seeing you at half past, then?'

Less than half an hour that was. Less.

Still. 'I swear. I'll see you, then. Thank you for the opportunity.'

And, as I dropped the phone from my ear, I heard a tinny voice continue. I listened in.

'You don't want the address?'

I apologised. She told me the address. I repeated it back. I said goodbye. She wished me luck. I thanked her. As I returned the phone, Jennifer asked what the plan was.

'We've less than half an hour to get to Melrose Avenue,' I said.

Jennifer's smile turned upside down. 'Well, that's not going to happen. We've not moved in five minutes.'

How could I get so close but fail so massively? I didn't regret going to the prison, but Jennifer *had* kind of bigged it up like her dad was a hardened criminal. And there'd been a distinct lack of police trying to arrest her, like she'd said there'd be.

Which all meant that I now possessed 100 per cent determination to get to the studio. This wasn't just something I wanted. This was something I needed. We all tell ourselves stories to cope with disappointment but now that I was so close to making it, my whole body quivered with the terrible question: 'What if?'

Honestly, I realised now, I'd never get over the disappointment if I missed the shoot. I'd be forced to wear black every day for the rest of my life. I'd move schools. I couldn't face explaining it to them. I'd change my name. I'd burn all my Marvel merch. Because it wasn't Doctor Bong, after all, and my eyes pricked with spidey tears.

Don't cry. Don't cry.

'Open the glove compartment,' said Mr Lewis. Jennifer frowned, but did as instructed. Mr Lewis lowered his window. 'Hand me the light.'

And, miraculously, Jennifer's hand appeared holding the sort of lamp you'd see spinning on top of a black-and-white squad car. Her dad flicked a switch at its base and the insides began turning, a miniature lighthouse. It flooded the space red and blue. His left hand took the light, about the size of a snow globe, and he stretched to land it with a thump on the car roof above his driving seat.

'One of the perks of working in a correctional facility,' he said.

He flicked an indicator to move out of the stationary traffic and so pull into the bus lane.

'Half an hour, you say?' The engine revved aggressively. 'We'll be there in twenty.'

Waze

By now the sun had set. Its orange farewell was mirrored in miniature by the reddening fuzz of streetlights and road signs. Flashing red and blue against jealous drivers in stationary cars, we lasted in the bus lane for three minutes until rolling up to the rear of a bus. Its back was plastered with an advert for SMART WATER. I tried focusing on this to avoid the increasing dread.

'Open Waze,' said Mr Lewis with a violent finger at his daughter.

The bus crawled forward. We followed.

'I am, I am,' said Jennifer, squinting at the app. 'Here, take the next right.'

Travelling at ten miles an hour we pulled from the

bus's behind and entered a side street busier than the one we'd left.

Mr Lewis braked.

It wasn't only full of vehicles. There were people here too. The road was flanked on each side with long lines of huge trucks. In the narrow path between men in orange hard hats waved directions at a fleet of forklift trucks. Each one of these yellow surprises held slabs of stuff unloaded from the lorries.

'Where have you taken us?' asked Mr Lewis, wrists balanced on top of the steering wheel, palms flapping at the chaos ahead.

Obviously it was a warehouse district. These trucks unloaded into the buildings stalking either side of the road. It was the exact reverse of a short cut. It was a long addition.

'It looked okay,' said Jennifer. 'Blame Waze.'

'Waze is never wrong,' replied her dad.

A huge klaxon filled the air and made my shoulders jump nearly as high as the roof. I turned to see the huge silver grille of an articulated lorry, the sort that drives shipments of guns from the east coast to the west, filling the entire rear windscreen.

'Here goes nothing,' said Mr Lewis, putting his foot down.

We swept forward and at a speed ten times faster than was safe. Jennifer and I took turns to gasp as the car threaded, like a sewing needle, back and forth between the forklifts and lorries. Every so often, a hard-looking man, with biceps larger than my waist, would swear and raise a fist. Mr Lewis didn't care. It was like there was a rocket strapped to the car, like he couldn't stop if he wanted to.

How we got through the channel of trucks I'll never know, especially as we hit nobody or nothing.

I think.

At the end of the road there was a stack of cardboard boxes.

'I've always wanted to do this,' said Mr Lewis, and he steered the nose of the car to nudge them.

He'd watched too many films, supposing the boxes to be empty. Instead they held blackcurrant cordial or juice or something dark and sticky and a thick purple cloud splashed against Jennifer's side of the windscreen.

She shrieked.

'Damn,' said Mr Lewis, as the car continued. 'But how about that for expert driving?'

He turned his head for my approval. I stared past him. At the horror ahead.

'Stop!' screamed Jennifer and the front grille almost kissed the ground as Mr Lewis slammed the brakes.

In front of us, past a barrier gate, rushed a snub-nosed train engine, pulling a dozen thick rounded steel containers.

Its wheels screamed energy. The car rocked in its wake.

I wanted to say something like 'that was close', but I was too busy concentrating on not being sick and, anyway, I don't think my voice would have been heard over the beating of my heart, let alone the roar of the train.

When it had passed, the barriers rose.

'You want to take a left after the tracks,' said Jennifer, sounding like she might need a wee.

Mr Lewis did as suggested, turning back on to the same two-lane thoroughfare we'd started on, and just about missing a passing bus. Had he jumped a red light? I don't know, but it was our second near miss in about three minutes.

'I don't want to die,' I said.

I could see Jennifer's head nodding.

'Chill, Dad. It's no use if he gets to the studio dead.'

Mr Lewis wasn't chilling. After the close call with the train and bus, he ran another stop light and narrowly avoided a head-on collision with an ice-cream van. Mr

Whippy screamed swear words as we passed. We turned a corner, tyres squealing. The windows steamed up as we fought to keep our breath.

'Are we far off?' asked Mr Lewis as if he'd been motoring along at a grandmother speed, out for a spin in the country, the car's MPH now regular.

'Are you kidding me?' asked Jennifer. 'The studio's three minutes up this street.'

'There we go,' said Mr Lewis. 'No problem at all. Didn't I say I was going to get you here, Jacob, pal? Jacob? You okay? Yippee-ki-yay! Jacob?'

After some retching, I spoke. 'Where did you learn to drive like that?'

'Afghanistan, baby,' said Mr Lewis, and Jennifer rolled her eyes.

'He worked in an office,' she said.

CHAPTER 41

Paramount
Hollywood, Los Angeles, California

And, sure enough, a long wall painted white, and probably older than cinema, ran two stone arches: the entrance to the Paramount lot. Palm trees stretched up to the sky behind and tall lights, more studio than street, spread sparkling light across the scene.

Mr Lewis pulled over and, turning from the wheel, offered me his hand, losing his getaway driver persona and coming over all adult.

'Well, for all the twenty minutes I've known you, you seem like a good kid. So stay safe. And be careful with your cross-country adventures in future. You've my number if there's a problem. And I'll call the studio to check you're okay tonight. Got it?'

It really *was* goodbye. A camera flash of a memory

that I'd recall for the rest of my life. I just hoped I didn't ruin it by acting like an idiot and falling out of the car or crying or whatever.

'Break a leg,' said Jennifer. 'Is that what I'm meant to say?'

'Better a leg than a wrist,' I replied like a sad clown. Neither of the Lewises laughed. 'Come with me! Both of you! Please! You can park up and there won't be a problem because even if you can't actually go where the film's shooting I'm sure you could wait around and there's probably free coffee and I won't take long and I've said about my hotel, haven't I?'

I'd almost, with these frantic words, persuaded myself that all this might happen. The look on their faces showed I was wrong.

'Jennifer's wanted by police in five states,' said Mr Lewis.

'Seven,' said Jennifer.

'And I'm turning this car round and taking her straight to the airport. You've heard about her grandmother, right? A bona fide Lex Luthor.'

I went to open the door.

'Wait!' Jennifer undid her seat belt. Her dad fussed but she didn't care. 'I want to say thank you.' A car sounded. We were blocking the entrance. 'So thank you.'

We stretched arms through the awkward space. We

hugged. Jennifer could probably smell the thousands of miles we'd travelled but didn't complain. Neither did I. My eyes stung but that was probably the smog in LA because the air quality wasn't great, to be honest.

'I've got the spending money due. I could fly back to see you. To Chicago,' I said, Captain Cringe.

'I'm not going back to Chicago.'

'Jennifer . . .' growled her dad.

'The only reason she put me in that sucky school is that I didn't have any parents, Dad.'

'You've got me now.'

'I know. That's my point.'

My cheeks flushed because I was intruding on one of those serious family conversations – the strange flashes of parents telling kids the truth.

'Monday, you're back at school. You finish the term. Then we can talk about you moving out here,' said Mr Lewis. His tone softened. 'Look, I've spoken to Charlotte about it. Already. Before you even took this . . . trip.'

'Really?' Jennifer's face shone. 'For real? What did she say?'

'She said we'll talk about it. She said there were schools in LA. Let's let Jacob do what he's got to do and then we'll talk, okay?'

It was Mr Lewis's turn to get a hug from Jennifer. Looking at me over her shoulder, he rolled his eyes in the exact way she always did.

'I'd better be going, then,' I said in a tiny voice as the car behind sounded its horn again. Longer and, if it's possible, louder this time.

'Bye, then,' said Jennifer. 'Have a good life, I guess.'

'We'll see each other again,' I said. 'I swear.'

'I know,' she said. 'I'm messing.'

Now there came actual shouting from the car behind us. Bad words. *GTA* words. Those words.

A security guard stepped from the entrance, dressed in a coplike uniform that looked like it had been borrowed from the costume department. He pulled up his belt and walked towards us. He had those big reflective sunglasses you see in all the shows set in LA.

'Don't forget the cash I gave you,' said Jennifer.

'What cash?' asked Mr Lewis, but he was ignored.

Jennifer continued. 'And, Jacob Bowser Jacob, I remember your email. But mainly don't forget the cash. Check it before you pay for anything.'

I nodded like I understood.

The car behind sounded its horn again. Three loud toots. *And* the driver shouted. He'd be in for a surprise if he

285

wanted to argue with Mr Lewis. You don't go hooting at ex-soldiers, I'm telling you. Anyway, the security guard was at our bonnet and he had his arms outstretched, indicating like he wanted to know what the hell the problem was.

'By the way, there are a few people you might need to pay back, Pops,' said Jennifer, smiling at me. 'We borrowed some dollar.'

I pulled at the door release. It creaked open and I stepped out, lifting the Princess with me.

'What is this? Amateur hour?' shouted a man's voice from behind us.

Jennifer wound down her window. She offered a middle finger at the shouty man. Mr Lewis complained . . . but laughed at the same time.

'It was fun,' she said to me. 'We should do it again sometime.'

A long screech of horn tore through the air. Jennifer hadn't made the guy any less angry. Mr Lewis set his car going and Jennifer swung away from me like a stone cast spinning across water: bouncing, bouncing, bouncing.

'What's the problem here?' asked the security guard.

'Nothing. I was saying goodbye.'

CHAPTER 42

Fame and Fortune

Seven minutes they had me. The extras walked through a set in the studio backlot that was meant to look like New York. There were bricks and fire hydrants. A camera moved down the middle of the fake street on a track. Its operator sat up on a chair sticking out in the air. And she, the operator, filmed us extras. Walking through New York, acting.

This was done twice. Each for three and a half minutes. And then we were thanked and we were led to an outside space, under canvas umbrellas, lit by floodlights, where we had our make-up removed. Next we stood in shower cubicles made of fabric to get changed from our extras' costumes into our own clothes. (Which was kind of embarrassing because I'd still not had a shower.) As I got undressed, I thought about Jennifer. It was great that she was going to stay in LA with her dad. Really great.

And despite it being really great, really, really great, I couldn't shake this huge feeling of disappointment, like I was wearing a cloak of misery.

'The good thing about this kind of scene,' said an old woman who'd been given a dog to walk, 'is that they always need them in the final piece. Establishing location. It's when you've got the majors speaking dialogue out front that you're risking the cut.'

I asked a make-up woman, one who looked like she had a massive Insta following, if it would be okay if I could go to the bathroom.

'You don't have to ask permission, darling,' she said, and for a second I thought she might hug me.

'Could you tell me where they are, please?'

Smiling like I was a kitten, which I'm not, she pointed to a hut leaning against the side of one of the huge warehouses in which they make the movies, I guess.

It looked like the temporary classroom where I stared out of the window for three years of RS lessons. Inside a cramped corridor there were three doors. One said WRITERS' ROOM, the others led to male and female toilets. I could hear strange noises coming out of the gents from outside. It was a grunting, like an animal was dreaming.

It didn't matter. I really needed a slash. I pushed through the door. Guess what was there? Yes – a row of urinals and a sink – a cubicle too, but also:

SPIDER-MAN!

Or, at least, someone in a Spider-Man costume, their back turned. The mask wasn't on, the back of their head was full of black hair. Their hands, covered in the red and blue spidey fabric, were turned at a weird angle to grab at a zip. The suit, you see, wasn't fully *on*. It hadn't been zipped up, breaking to reveal a V shape of skin from the shoulders down.

'Lucy? Is that you?'

Spider-Man turned. I gasped. I won't pretend I didn't – because . . . it was him. For real. A, like, genuine Hollywood actor. He was shorter than I imagined but he had the same face I'd seen acting in Marvel movies, the same face I'd seen in the Wellesley Cinema, back in Somerset. Pretty much exactly the same face, actually.

'I'm not Lucy,' I said. 'Sorry about that.' He nodded. 'But I'm Jacob. And I won a competition. Thank you.'

'Never apologise for not being Lucy,' he replied.

I was so excited I couldn't stop talking. I told him all

about Somerset, the competition, the mad journey, the poem, which I even offered to recite but, sorry, he was pushed for time, which was completely understandable.

'And I met this girl called Jennifer and she was out of this world.'

He asked what scene I'd been in. He said it sounded 'crap'. He said they'd get me in one with him at the very least.

'Wow,' I said. 'Thanks,' I said.

He nodded. He said it wasn't a problem. He said Brits had to stick together. He said that Jennifer sounded like quite the individual.

CHAPTER 43

Sharpie
Chicago, Illinois

A day later, I was sitting in a departure lounge at Chicago O'Hare airport. The flight from LA had been so dull I'd slept through an Avengers movie. Now I watched a boyfriend and girlfriend argue about a lost wallet.

I'd rung home. I'd told them I'd made it to the film in time. I told them about the scene with Spider-Man. To say they were excited would be an understatement. Well, Mum and Dad were, at least.

What the director had me do, and the actual director, was walk along the same fake New York street from earlier. This time, though, just as I was about to fall down an open manhole cover, Spider-Man shot out some web and saved me. The manhole cover and web and most of everything else on the street would be added in 'post-production', so it reminded me a bit of one of those drama lessons that was heavy on pretending and light on props and scenery, but . . . still . . . actual Spider-Man. My hands didn't stop shaking for hours afterwards. He'd hugged me and said I should think about acting because he'd seen loads of extras and I was okay.

'He actually said "okay",' I said.

'Good job, son,' said Dad. 'What a star.'

'He called you "okay"?' asked Mum.

We arranged meeting at Heathrow. The thought filled the world with grey. Even the name of the airport sounded dull. Heath. Row. So English. So boring. And Dad told me not to miss my connecting flight.

I couldn't get to sleep that night in the Hollywood Roosevelt. I was still excited about the shoot and if I said I didn't check the selfie I'd taken of Spider-Man with his arm round my shoulders maybe a hundred times, I'd be lying.

But . . . I think the real problem was the bed. There was nothing uncomfortable about it. It was, in fact, the most comfortable bed I'd ever been in. It was like the mattress instantly knew every curve of your body and supported you like a giant's hand. No. It's . . . I'd got kind of used to sleeping on buses. This here didn't feel like me.

Where's Jennifer? I thought when I woke.

But she wasn't there. She was back in Chicago with her wicked grandmother.

Someone from Marvel picked me up in the morning. They said they were an intern and when they'd applied for the position they never thought it would involve childcare. I laughed like they were joking, which I don't think they were.

Their last words were: 'Don't miss your flight this time, Jason.'

'Your attention, please. Passengers for United flight UA968 to London, boarding will begin at Gate C15.'

I stood up. The Princess waited at my feet like an ugly but attentive dog. In the same jeans I'd been wearing all week I pulled out the money Jennifer had given me. I wanted to buy water and sweets before leaving America, but *didn't* want to crack open the Marvel cash.

A week's worth of spending money unspent. Add it to Jennifer's and maybe I could buy a laptop? To Skype on.

And I remembered what she'd said before she'd left: 'Check it before you pay for anything.'

And so I did.

Zwap! Pow! Whamm!

She'd written, in a thick black marker, on a fifty-dollar note. What had she written? Her address in Chicago.

What next?

I'm not saying it was a particularly original idea. It definitely wasn't one that needed a load of thought. But as I stood there, faced with the decision to do the right thing, the thing Mum and Dad would want me to do, and the wrong thing, leaving the airport to find Jennifer's house, I knew that there was only one way that this was ever going to end.

England could wait. Me and the Princess were going to surprise Jennifer. Just a flying visit. A cup of tea and a slice of cake. As small an adventure as there could be.

Because there'd be flights to Heathrow tomorrow. I wouldn't even miss school. Because America had taught me that sometimes the wrong decision's the *best* decision. Because now my story had come to an end, I realised that I didn't need to be a superhero. Being a teenager who wasn't afraid of getting in a bit of trouble now and again was exciting enough.

That said, I'd probably not take a bus to Jennifer's school. I'd try a taxi this time.

Read on for a sample of
Tom Mitchell's first book,
How to Rob a Bank . . .

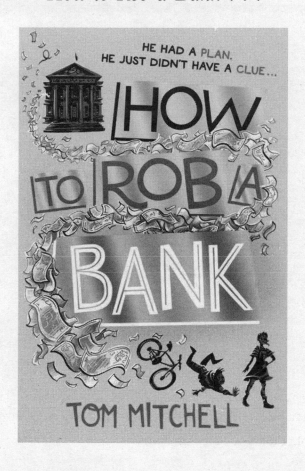

Short-term Pain for Long-term Gain

The man wore a corporate tie and a black rectangular name badge. It announced him to be 'Max Gradual', the branch manager. I took all this in while raising myself from a kneeling position, as if having just been knighted, and I said, *Yes, all was okay and I was going home now, so*—

The automatic doors shivered open, even though there was nobody close. I turned to watch their movement, then realised that this made me look suspicious as if I were contemplating running off, which I was.

'I've been watching you, young man,' said Gradual. 'You seem very interested in our cash machines.'

I felt the force of an audience: the old couple, the woman with the buggy – they'd forgotten why they'd come to the bank. Their reason for being was now me.

'I'm doing a school project,' I said. 'On cash machines.'

Gradual nodded. He smiled like he was about to bite. His teeth were coffee-coloured.

'A project, eh?' he said. 'A project? A project about cash machines? Tell me about your project about cash machines. Maybe we'll be able to help with your project about cash machines. A project! I love projects. And these *are* cash machines.'

The kid in the buggy began crying. His mum fussed to find a dummy. The kid was silenced.

'It's for English,' I said and regretted my subject choice. Of all my GCSEs, English was a poor choice for a cash machine project. Although, I could have chosen French, which would have been worse because I don't know the French for cash machine. *Machine d'argent?* I don't know the French for most things.

'So what were you looking for? How can I help? With your project?'

The manager stared me down with such intensity that I could see the tiny threads of blood appear in the whites of his eyes. And his voice: he'd barked, he'd properly barked. But . . . his words, his questions . . . was he trying to help? Did I dare ask about USB slots? I mean, I'd not done anything wrong. I'd looked at his cash machines. It was because I was a teenager. In his middle-aged, slightly scary eyes, my age meant I was trouble. And that's prejudice.

'It doesn't matter,' I said as I heard the automatic doors hiss open again and decided I'd take the sound as a prompt to leave.

'What's up?'

My sister's voice. And she was standing next to me. Still looking like an evil athlete in her all-black get-up. But not in the car. *Good job I got a ticket*, I thought.

'I'm Max Gradual, branch manager. Who are you?'

'I'm this kid's sister. What's the problem?'

'Give the boy a break,' said the old woman. The room's focus turned to her. 'He wasn't doing anything wrong, were you, love? Crawling about, that's all. For his project.'

I bit my bottom lip like I was a cute toddler or something. Gradual straightened his back an increment, no longer bending over to pin me down with his stare.

'Did you ask him?' Rita asked me.

She couldn't. Was she? I mean, she knew this was a mistake. It was obvious it was a mistake. All this. What was I ever thinking? You can't be asking about the security of USB ports. It's all about the secrecy.

The woman with the baby spoke. She wasn't queuing any longer; there was nobody at the cashier's window. The fat businessman had left without me noticing and the cashier, a young woman who might be fit, stared at the action through the glass, resting her possibly fit face in her hand.

'He said he was doing a project. Didn't you?' said the mother.

I nodded. Because that's exactly what I'd said.

Gradual's eyes darted around the space to meet the gaze of the audience: the old couple, the mother, the cashier, Rita. He attempted a smile, which looked more like he was reacting to having his privates placed in a vice.

'He didn't ask for a job? He was meant to ask for a job,' said Rita. 'You were meant to ask for a job.'

Gradual shook his head. I shook my head. My mouth was suddenly dry. I wanted to tell Rita that we should leave. I wanted to tell Rita that I didn't want a job. We could be unemployed together. But I'd need a glass of water to do that.

'We're not hiring,' said the manager. 'And how old are you? I thought you were at school. Doing your project.'

His tone had shifted. He was on the defensive.

'Give the boy a job,' said the old man.

'Saturday morning,' said Rita. 'A schoolboy trainee. You're open Saturday mornings, right? The thing is, ever since our parents died, we've struggled for money and not only that but the discipline and organisation required to work in such an obviously well-run bank is just what the boy needs. I said our parents were dead, didn't I?'

Things were unravelling. Like the life status of Mum and Dad. What if I ran outside? The people would forget about us. They'd think it was a joke. I could deal with Rita later. I wasn't yet an adult. I was well within my rights, and expectations of fifteen-year-olds' behaviour, to run away.

But my feet didn't move. I was rooted to the carpet.

'They're open Saturday morning,' said the mother and the cashier nodded behind her. 'You poor children. Give the boy a chance.'

'So sad,' said the old man. 'Go on. A Saturday job.'

Allegiances shifted. Suddenly Gradual was my only ally in the room. We were united in not wanting me to work here. Not least because I was planning to rob the place, not that he knew that. It was all very well for Rita in her Nike Death outfit, but I'd be the first person they'd suspect when the cash went missing: the ace teenager recently hired, having been discovered inspecting the cash machines and claiming he was doing a school project. He'd always been so quiet, so friendly.

'I don't know,' I said, looking down at my dirty Converse.

'I don't know,' said Gradual, looking down at his sensible leather shoes.

'We have the part-time school-age temp scheme,' called the cashier, offering a thumbs up.

'The poor boy,' said the old man. 'An orphan.'

'Well, I'd need to see your CV,' said Gradual. 'And your parents really are dead?'

'Umm,' I said because my parents, as far as I knew, weren't dead.

'Yes,' said Rita. 'Really dead. Completely dead.'

'My parents have passed away too. An accident up Ben Nevis. Look, what's your name?'

'I'm not sure . . .' I began.

'Dylan,' said Rita.

'Dylan,' said Gradual. 'Maybe we'll be able to find you something. It just so happens our part-time school-age temp recently left us.' There were muted cheers around the bank branch. 'But being in school doesn't mean we don't expect you to work hard. On the contrary.'

'Thank you so much,' said Rita. 'We'll email you his details.'

'My email's on the website. Or drop it round. Whatever's easiest.'

He'd said 'whatever's easiest'. This was a deep change in the man who was bellowing at me three minutes earlier. Gradual didn't seem like a 'whatever's easiest' type of guy.

'Thanks again,' said Rita, grabbing the manager's hand and shaking it wildly. He stood dazed. 'Shake his hand,' she said to me, releasing her grip.

'Well, I'll need to see his CV first. And a covering letter. And the Saturday position is more training than job, so it won't pay much.'

He was speaking for the sake of the audience. He was trying to wrestle control from Rita. It had been simpler for him before she'd turned up. Simpler for me too.

But I did as I was told. I shook his hand. I said thanks. And we left. A wave to the cashier, the mother, the two OAPs.

Inside the car, buckling my safety belt, I asked Rita what had just happened.

'I got you access, that's what,' she said. 'You're our insider.'

'I don't want to work there, Rita. I'm fifteen and I've got GCSEs to do.'

'I don't *want* an ungrateful brother, but some things you've just got to put up with. Did you check the colour of the guy's teeth? Gross.'

She started the engine and reversed the car out of the parking bay. A passing Range Rover sounded its horn but Rita didn't react.

I thought back to what Dad had said about how being an adult was coping with a succession of people telling you to do things you don't want to do.

'How did you know the machines didn't have USB slots?' I asked. 'You came in banging on about our parents being dead and getting me a job, but you never asked about the USB slots.'

'Don't be an idiot all your life.'

All right, I thought, feeling the heat of my blood increase by a degree, *I'll take your job. And you know what else I'll do? I'll rob the bank of tens, maybe hundreds, of thousands of pounds and then we'll see who's the idiot when you're begging me to buy you a MacBook Air.*

And, I reasoned, even if everything went wrong and

the bank never got robbed, at least I'd have earned some cash. I could buy Beth one of those tiny mirrors that women have in their purses. That'd be a sensitive gift. It could have a little jewelled whale design. It would show I understood women. Unlike Harry, for instance. And, you know, it might not be thousands of pounds and it might not compensate her for burning down her house or pay for a deposit, but, as Mum says every Christmas, it's the thought that counts.

'Whatever,' I said to Rita. 'What. Ever.'

At least Mum and Dad would be pleased. About me getting a job.

ACKNOWLEDGEMENTS

With thanks to my amazing agent, Lauren Abramo, and her awesome London representative, Anna Carmichael. I'm extremely lucky to have such a talented editor in Harriet Wilson; all the thanks too to her. Where would I be without Harriet's alchemy? Further gratitude is due to Julia Sanderson, Sean Williams, and everyone else at HarperCollins Children's. I'm also extremely grateful to the Society of Authors. Their grant enabled me to journey across America, albeit without missing any flights.

ABOUT THE AUTHOR

Tom Mitchell is mostly a dad, partly a teacher and sometimes a writer. He grew up in the West Country and settled in London after a brief interlude in the East Midlands. *How to Rob a Bank* was his first novel, written in the school holidays, and *That Time I Got Kidnapped* is his second. He lives in the People's Republic of Orpington with his wife, Nicky, and sons, Dylan and Jacob.